REACH
DON BAJEMA

ISBN# 1-880985-19-5

Illustrations: David Eggers

Design: **ENDLESS** ∞

2.13.61
P.O. BOX 1910 · LOS ANGELES ·
CALIFORNIA · 90078 · USA

2.13.61

P.O. BOX 1910 · LOS ANGELES · CALIFORNIA · 90078 · USA

2.13.61 Info Hotline: (213) 969-8043

Contents

LET US PRAY

Somewhere between a fight and a dance is the mystery of our true spirit. A secret that can turn moments into a history fit for human consumption. To let time nourish instead of erode, to let time nourish instead of erode, to let time nourish instead of erode. To let time nourish instead of erode.

SPILT MILK

Pelican Bay up above San Francisco is dicey with its visitation rights. I'd drive up from Topanga Canyon to be told the population is locked down and they'd send me home. Like today. I'm playing the Jerry Lee Lewis live at the Hamburg Star Club tape I intended to give Uncle Pete Burnett. A styrofoam cup of brown-water coffee from a Chevron station wedged against my balls. Driving south, thinking about 1961 up in the farm country on the Washington-Canadian border.

My father and mother had just shown up and were getting ready to take me back to Southern California when the feud between the Hoeks and the Burnetts finally got deadly. Like most things that have long term consequences, it keeps you wondering how it could have happened. I mean there had been about six other incidents that could have left someone dead. It was a forgone conclusion that something was going to happen someday. And then when it did, you never saw it coming. Things just got out of hand, I guess.

The men in the Hoek family down the road were either moon-faced, perpetually red and sweaty, huge and dumb, or like a cartoon rat, hatchet-faced fucks. They tried to play themselves off as practical jokers and bad asses. Everyone up there knew them. Well, they knew us too, but people didn't spit on the street after we passed, or leave the bar when the Burnett men walked in.

The Hoeks were nine families of nine brothers. We had eight brothers and their families plus four sisters and theirs. Most of the Dutch farms on the Northwestern Canadian border had big families. It wasn't all that unusual.

Two of the Hoek brothers cheated my father's best friend out of a tractor in high school and got the county to quarantine my uncle Ray's herd for six months by spreading a rumor about a sick calf he said he had to kill, one that Uncle Ray sold him. It took two quarantined months of dumping milk and taking blood samples to prove that there was nothing wrong with his herd. If it weren't for his brother Sam, Ray would have lost his farm.

The Hoeks made you feel you'd been insulted. It was in their yellow stained sneers and smoky breath. The way they'd slink, while their eyes grinned an accusation of stupidity or cowardice at you. They didn't want to get into anything real with my uncles. It was just constant hot air and bullshit. They never really came right out with anything you could build a conflict over. It was sneaky, "good-natured" stuff that just made the world a lot less pleasant. They were universally despised and they reveled in it.

They also had five of the nine brothers on the six-time Washington State Men's Championship Softball Team. They got lots of beer bought for them, and they were able to take advantage of hundreds of hicks who never saw pitching and hitting like theirs, from Yakima to Everett to the Columbia Gorge. They sold unusable aluminum siding, cheated in pool halls and blackmailed a drunk with a wealthy family near Bellingham. The rats played infield, while one of the fat giants pitched and the other one caught.

Mom and I were sitting in the International with Dad eating donuts in front of the thrift store when two Hoeks, a shortstop and a giant too big to play, named "Three Ball" because of his huge red nose, passed our truck. We pretended not to see the squinty little glance or notice the huge pair of overalls walking sideways and forward at the same time. Mom and I were sure they weren't gonna say anything with my dad there.

The giant looked at the rat who was looking at us, who then looked back at the giant as he ripped off the loudest fart I had ever heard. Their eyes shot into the truck cab and the rat started to squeak out a laugh which he pretended to cover with an apology. My father already had my donut and was grabbing my mother's and opening the cab door muttering how he believed we've lost our goddamn appetite, and then fired the donuts at the head of the rat.

They stood to their full height as my father flew up to them. They were making eye contact with witnesses and acting like responsible citizens who were confused and outraged by my dad's unprovoked assault. They hadn't taken into consideration that my father had stayed up for two nights with an abscessed tooth which was yanked yesterday, had a Rainier Ale headache, and had just been arguing with my Mom.

Dad stood between them, dwarfed by the giant who was pulling a ratchet out his back pocket. The rat muttered something to him. Dad rose up on his toes while Mom was saying to herself, "Oh, no." Then he clocked the giant with a solid fist to his jack-o-lantern head. One of his huge boots started to lift off the ground as he listed to one side. Dad hit him again and the giant fell and rolled over on his hip. The rat had his knife out, demanding to know what the fuck was my dad doing—for the benefit of the witnesses.

My mother was screaming about my father's parole, and the rat was backing up as my Uncle Pete came out of the thrift store with a hydraulic jack. The giant was trying to lift his stomach off the ground high enough to get his knees under him. Pete stood over him and the giant stayed down, pretending he was having a delayed reaction to Dad's punches.

The rat started talking about calling the law and what trash our family was, and how lucky Dad was he didn't cut him up right now. To which my father replied, "Come on."

The rat swung the knife around in the air, moving in on my dad. A few spectators began to make noises. My father was talking quietly telling the rat that if he got the knife, he was gonna show him a couple things he didn't know about yet.

I was so embarrassed. All this right out in town for church people to talk about. All the thriftstore shoppers, mouths open, smelling like piss from going through the clothes racks. Holding broken toys and useless appliances in their hands, staring out the fly-spotted windows, hoping to see something real awful to talk about for a few weeks. And my dad, white with rage and staring bug-eyed, jumping like a matador while the rat swung toward him. Dad showing no sense whatever. Mom getting mad, yelling, "Go ahead you fool! If you think it's worth it!" She'd tell Dad on the ride home she was yelling at the rat. But I saw her face, I knew what she meant. Dad was losing it again.

The rat put the knife away and strutted around in a circle, making face-saving threats as my dad got in the truck. He drove us home with Uncle Pete and my mom in the cab and me riding with our dog in the truck bed. I watched them argue. Mom taking it from both sides. When we parked in front of the house and the doors swung open, Uncle Pete told my dad that Sam heard the Hoeks been jack-lighting deer over near our place.

Two nights later I was trying to conceal from my two uncles the effort it took to keep up with their long strides. It meant walking as fast as I could, then jogging along, then walking, then skipping into a run again. It was their hunting pace; they weren't going to slow up. Pete was a little clumsy, so I'd have to make sure to give him plenty of room or he'd poke me with the end of his bow and hiss, "Stay out from under my goddamn feet."

We'd covered about half a mile toward the back road behind the farm. Behind me the silos loomed in shadow. The barn and farmhouse were dark shapes squatting on the ground. The next time I looked back, I saw nothing but tiny stars.

Sam let his brother lead. It was as though he had invisible reins attached to Pete. Pete would wear the face of a man in control of serious events. But he'd stop when it came to creek crossings or changes in the terrain. He'd wait and Sam would mutter or grunt, and Pete would make his decision, always in favor of Sam's advice, and plunge ahead. Pete would pretend to think during the pause when Sam was actually thinking. Pete'd turn slow circles and rub his neck. He would pretend to offer a suggestion or opinion, but long ago he had learned his stated views were sources of embarrassment for him. So he would get the "light bulb" look on his face and then slowly scowl and "change" his mind in silence. If Sam pondered something for more than ten minutes, Pete would pull his-idea-no-never-mind act five or six times. It made me grind my teeth. His dull eyes would squint at me. I was twelve now and had begun openly risking the result of shaking my head at him in disgust. This was acceptable within the family, if it didn't undermine Pete's position as one of the Burnett brothers in public.

Sam always had his mind set on action. He completed what was before him then moved on to the next thing. In a day's chores on his farm, you could see that Sam planned for the future. He saw the workings of each day and adjusted the rate and sequence of chores, completing more of them than any man I knew. Sam's crops were rotated to market price, livestock thrived. His disposition was even and his judgments were fair. He had a practical patience with life.

You'd think as close as they were, all the brothers would see more of each other. But they had sort of paired up according to their ages. Sam and Pete were a year apart. While Sam had made a name for himself, Pete was widely considered a fool. Sam handled Pete as one would a ferocious dog—affectionate and firm. Right now they were both absolutely pissed off.

We were crossing our longest pasture, kicking up and slipping on cow pies here and there, soaking wet above our boots whenever we crossed off the path. Pete asked Sam why the hell did I have to come anyway.

"Because his father is in jail."

"So?"

"So he has to be here."

We walked in silence for a couple hundred yards. Pete started in on how I always brought up questions about what made people tick. His head spun on his long neck and his face dropped about two feet out of the sky, one eye cocked and squinting at me. It was malevolence designed to instruct. He did not want anyone figuring him out before he had a chance. He thought he had secrets. Jesus, I thought he was stupid. A throwback to a line that could not have survived without tolerant assistance from brothers like Sam. Pete hissed at Sam. Did he think I could keep my mouth shut? Sam shrugged.

"Ask him. Don't ask me."

They sped up unconsciously to get some distance from the irritation between them. I trotted behind Sam.

Pete pushed it saying, "Well...?" in a tone that demanded an answer.

I did not say a word.

At the same instant, Sam and Pete stopped in a fraternal choreography worked out over thirty-odd years of stalking game. Frozen mid-stride, mid-breath, mid-heartbeat for no reason other than something they automatically understood between them. They towered above me, posed like shadow conjurers. The scimitar moon staked over Sam's shoulder, reflecting the silver in the strands of his long gray hair. Pete put his finger to the side of his nose and fired a clot of hay fever in a heavy wad out of his head, missing me by about a foot. Whatever had stopped them was now permitting them to move. Sam had already disappeared.

"Well can ya?" Pete moved to grab me as I followed Sam.

Sam stopped. It was time to get Pete's mind off this issue. He walked out of the dark and stood over me, his head turned to the side and looking out of one eye. He had always looked like a bird. The moon backlit his profile, his nose beaked like an Egyptian drawing I'd seen of a man with a hawk head. Pete felt he had a confederate in Sam in the demand that I answer.

Pete shifted his balance and cleared his throat. I got ready to duck. He asked again.

"Eddie, can you keep your mouth shut? I'm not talking about little jerkoff secrets now. I mean you gotta be able to..."

Sam interrupted him by turning his eyes on him.

I looked at Pete like I had no idea what he was talking about.

I heard the baritone growling up from the snot in Pete's throat which usually preceded violence.

Sam sounded disgusted from the dark.

"I guess his mouth is shut."

I could hear the long grass whisking his jeans as he moved on. Pete looked at me.

"I don't want you answering nobody's questions. You ain't here."

He examined me up close for the slightest sign of sass. I looked at the ground around me. We started walking again.

I was tired of explaining the basic shit to my family and it seemed to me that now that I was twelve, if I didn't stop doing it, I'd be explaining myself to somebody for the rest of my life. I relied on the Sams of the world to see the obvious and not have to tell it to them again and a goddamned again. I wanted to deal with people who had ideas of their own, not those asking for answers and explanations from somebody else. It looked like a fairly lonely ratio but I was already past giving a shit.

Pete passed me in six steps. I ran along behind him. My uncles were gliding in something like a run—low, level, silent and real fast. We were gaining a lot of ground on the fifteen or so deer we were trailing. I thought I saw them, but I couldn't have, it was too dark. There was another sense at play, one I had no recollection of. It was just there as we ran over the pasture.

Our speed increased when we dipped into a deep grass ravine. Birds flushed. At the top of the opposite side we froze, three statues low in the field, pretending to be hallucinations, being I guess, psychologically invisible. It was part of a rhythm, a ritual of our ghostly northern clan—the hunt in the dark and all the hoodoo that goes with it. The connection with the night, the deer, my uncles, the rhythm, and the fact that I had somehow known when and how to freeze as they froze—all this burst a small dam of adrenaline inside me.

I stood there invisible with my uncles. A wave of energy passed over the field from a jittery doe. It hit my uncles; it hit me too. I felt a smile coming over my face. From the ground through our senses into our blood. We stopped and time stopped. And nobody was there but the deer. The three of us had changed into something else through the energy of standing motionless. Until that moment I thought hunting was pursuit and killing. What it is—is infiltration. Because the deer forgot about us, they moved closer and broke their own perimeter, putting us just inside the herd. We'd crossed the line that would normally have made them run, and the deer, lacking imagination, figured we couldn't be there. Like magic.

And since my dad got busted for drunk driving and they held him over the weekend because he needed to cool off, I was his representative in the spell we had on the deer. I was being initiated. Not through my uncles' intentions. Just because it happens that way.

We were out in our field heading for the cutoff road between town and the county line. A road driven by drunks—like my dad last night—and State Troopers. The blacktop crossed at the far end of our northern pasture. I'd been thinking the whole time we were hunting deer. But when we started to move again it didn't seem like it.

Sam was the best archer in the entire Pacific Northwest. These deer were "gimmes" as far as his aim and the power of his bow was concerned. Pete was almost as good as Sam. We stood within a herd of deer with eight-point bucks almost close enough to spit on, and neither man had nocked an arrow on his string.

It was more like we were driving the herd instead of setting it up to get shots. Sam kept up the pressure, closing space on them enough to move them, but not enough to get them to run. Just very subtle suggestions in the way Sam leaned would be enough to shift the herd. It was like a dance between us, and in the next half hour we must have moved them a half mile. By the time we had them near our fence line we stopped, and I listened to them cropping the grass and snuffling. I either smelled them or imagined it; I couldn't tell.

Three cars dotted the distance. One of them broke free of the other two and began to unwind down the road. As the light went from stars to the shimmer of starlight, the deer went from invisible shadows to outlines, and as the car growled steadily beyond, they froze. The headlights passed, the shimmer wiped away and the taillights burned smaller and smaller.

I knew the terrain well enough from walking it every summer. Although it was black as pitch out there, fingernail moon or not, I knew the ground beneath me. I was connected to the ground beneath me.

I unconsciously started to move. Sam put his hand on my arm to stop me. The deer broke and then settled. Sam pointed at his eye and whispered.

"They almost see us."

Sam put me in a headlock and slowly pulled me down on the grass, breathing in my ear.

"Deer see in the dark. That's what the Hoeks is banking on. Blindin' them with their car lights, then shooting them when they's helpless."

I was freezing in the wet dew. We laid there for what seemed like a hour. The deer snorting and stamping, cropping and blowing. That and silence.

Two more cars passed by, trying to approximate the speed limit and stay in their lanes.

Sam put his mouth over my ear and whispered, "The Hoeks are gonna have a hunting accident."

I got scared right there laying on my belly, the world of men had gotten a little too heavy for me.

Sam got up to his feet, flanked the herd and moved it closer to the corner fence. Pete flanked the far side and I stayed where I was.

Two cars raced down the road and a third pair of headlights lingered behind. The first two cars accelerated and became taillights. But the third pair of lights cut out. I could still hear the engine in the distance. The sound stopped at one of our cattle crossings and then started into the field, coming our way.

Pete hissed, "Them sons of bitches is on our land."

You didn't have to see his face to know what he looked like. I would not have wanted to be a Hoek for all the deer in Watcom County.

The truck was purring toward us in the dark. I heard a voice and the deer nearest me looked back in its direction. The truck killed its engine and rolled. I heard the heel of a boot thud on the side of a fender and a drunken, burping laugh. I saw the truck looming toward us with a figure sitting above each fender.

Then the high beams flashed, illuminating several of the herd around me. Two deer facing me looked side to side with ears bent backward and took off. They went into the air in a single spring and landed eight feet away. They launched again and disappeared. Three others stared into the headlights and were frozen. I saw their chests heaving and the smoke of their breath fanning in the white light. A gun blast from the truck rocked one to its side and it dropped in the grass.

Sam was running like a ghost along the edge of the headlight's glare in the distance. Pete disappeared in a low ravine.

Sam stopped. He pulled his bow in the dark and a dart zipped toward the truck. A man on a fender yelped, and I heard the echoing of the truck hood as he banged around on it.

The men in the truck started howling. One of them was doing a crazy dance in the headlights; I could see his arm pinned against his chest. Another arrow knocked him down.

"Oh, Jesus! Oh, Jesus!"

A man went into the headlights and fired several shots in even spacing, from one end of the light to the other. I heard a pop over my head, like the air had cracked.

One deer remained in the light standing like a lawn decoration. The man on the ground was yelling and thrashing. The men in the truck were screaming. The driver was grinding gears into reverse. A man stood in the light, his shadow cast long and short as the headlights bounced. He fired off more rounds in our general direction.

Pete was yelling, "Don't, don't, don't!"

But Sam wouldn't listen.

Sam's arrow hit the man with the gun in the knees and he threw his arms in the air. One of the Hoeks jumped out of the truck and tried to pull his fallen brother to the truck. The man yelled.

"Don't move me! Don't move me!"

This in time with the "don'ts" Pete was yelling. It became a kind of duet. One of Sam's arrows went through the windshield and the driver hit the gas in reverse. The tires whined in the grass.

Why the troopers were coming I don't know, but they were. Lights spinning and sirens blaring.

Pete said, "Oh, shit."

In a second or two, Sam was over and beyond me and with Pete.

The troopers were stopped at our cattle crossing and were on their way in.

Pete had Sam around the neck and was spitting words through his clenched teeth. Sam was trying to push him away. I ran up to them as though I had a purpose, but I couldn't do anything but watch Pete work his way behind Sam, his elbow viced around his neck. Sam was trying to throw him off and Pete jerked Sam's feet off the ground the whole time saying, "Do what I tell ya. Do what I tell ya."

They didn't have handcuffs for all of us. I rode in the front seat between two troopers. Pete and Sam rode in the back seat. An ambulance was supposed to be on the way, but one of the brothers died before it got there.

Pete said he'd done the shooting and Sam had tried to stop him. Pete said he'd do it again so they might as well put him away right now.

The trooper driving said, "I believe you are gonna get your wish."

Pete got life.

His seven brothers, four sisters and their families went to see him on his birthday the first year. We've kept that tradition for the most part, but over the years, five brothers have died, and the divorces and what all, has limited the number. I've been remiss. I've seen him twice in seven years. We write, once in a while. It gets hard to keep things in common. Him in a time capsule and us outside getting the wear and tear. He reads a lot.

Sam got elected to Congress until the Republicans took over.

He never missed Pete's birthday. Sam died in 1981. I think it nearly killed Pete to miss the funeral.

Last time I saw him, I went with my father. Dad hadn't seen him in a long while. I guess after a time, men aren't afraid to show what they feel. For most of the couple hours, they stood in each other's arms, laughing and talking quietly in a corner.

I sat smoking in the day room, watching the men around me trying to get comfortable with children they weren't raising and women they couldn't have. A teenager would saunter in, reluctant, hoping Dad would be cool, which they almost always were. Cool, controlled, nodding. Fingers on chins, pants pressed, collars sharp, eyes clear. Looking at their sons growing up, becoming men, leaving them behind.

With my father waiting at the door and the guards getting impatient, I finally put the question to him.

"Why'd you say it was you?"

He looked at me from another planet, one with an orbit that spun out of time, accelerating at me until the years between us caught up.

Have you ever been smiled at by someone who knows much more than you? See Pete, his eyes wrinkled at the corners, his face worn and dignified, his mouth suppressing his smile.

"Aww, Eddie. Some get caught, some don't. You know that, don't cha?"

Before I could respond, his arms were around me. His cheek banging into mine. His old muscles still powerful.

Before I could respond, he released his grip, spun on his heel and walked to the impatient guard. His shoes were shined, his cuffs were low—an old man walking close to the earth.

Before I could respond, they closed the door behind him.

BEAR FLAG STATE

An expanse of giant thighs spread wide, thrusting and falling, spines snaking over the Central Valley horizon. Sierra's foothills rolling for three hundred miles in ecstasy beneath California's fiery sky.

Shasta stands white to the north.

The Pacific blasts cliffs from Big Sur to Mexico, prehistoric monsters stalk beneath the Red Triangle's shimmering surface.

The Mojave extends to the coast to the south. Sunset in summer brings euphoria as though the day were a dream changing below warm breezes and stars. Fertile plains lined with mossy ditches replace lakes and marshes. The winter blows arctic hail over valley floors, ice grips mountain peaks.

The dusk of August the tenth, seventeen ninety-two is hot. Heading south on El Camino Real, one hundred miles north of San Juan Bautista, are nine mounted churchmen recently from Spain, seventeen of Yerba Buena's garrison leading twenty-three mules, six wranglers, and thirty-four slaves from outposts near Shasta. The slaves are silent and caked in dust. Each male tied at each side to a female who are themselves tied to children. Young males are further discouraged from running having their elbows bound behind their back. Even so, the churchmen have blindfolded two males in sacks cinched at the neck. Two prepubescent girls tethered to an anguished priest. His lips work in silent repetition staring along the rolling ridges, becoming, to him, the inner thighs and the adjacent tendons jutting beside gaping valleys. His eyes follow the cracks undulating beneath the spines and heaving bellies defining his horizon.

Their worlds differ. Those in the dust see the plague of conquerors, replaced in the absence of their gods. Those aloft ride glory and purpose into the next century delivering order under the stern imperatives of their own Almighty. Each hoping their Heavenly Father will choose this time to bestow his long promised mercy.

These hour-upon-hours sway with the ripple of horses, creaking leather, and incessant whispering of this priest's pornographic mantras inhabiting his dark consciousness. The hills and the beast beneath, the bottomless eyes and unspoiled frames of these children become one thing. One huge anticipated desire for as much sin and raw perversion as he can possibly embrace in one night. Stolen away from camp where slaves are gagged and counted lost in the morning. He blinks as one girl's attempt to become invisible fails her. He turns away wondering how it is they always know.

The hours go on, the hillsides taunt obscenely before him. His eyes follow the round weight spilling from a golden giant whose curves lie still. Her leg draped over the shoulder of another asleep. Slowly the sun casts rocking shadows on his left and in his eye's corner he sees the dark shadow of the girls, the rolling haunches of his fabulous horse and his own body high above all. His shadow turns forward. A mule squalls and bucks its burden and suddenly as though dreaming, resumes his clopping gait.

These slaves will not labor. They are hopeless servants. Two decades of torture has taught them nothing. The mature females stare blindly in the heat, their feet bled dry running at any chance to return to their spot beneath a stand of oak trees. The males sit hunched refusing to see what is before their rage glistening eyes. The children try patience to the breaking point. Silent, sullen, seeming to owe their masters nothing, showing no effort other than ministering to those younger than themselves.

Even while on their knees in the shadow of God, they remain vacant, empty of any instruction, lost with the withering that precedes disease clouding deep within the vast depth of their eyes. They are good for very little for a very short period of time. Then in a single night they are lost. As though recalled into their savage ways. They resist. Whole villages die in numbers that can only stand as evidence of God's displeasure with them. Today driven with the mules to Mission San Diego. Given their last chance in the faint hope that distance will open their eyes and return them to their knees staring as they must into God's sky above.

Gusts of wind slant yellow fields of wild mustard, catching the traveler's clothes, winding them in the raising dust, swirling everything into disorder. Swimming through gritty tears the horses snort and stamp; the trailing mule squalls and plants its feet honking a series of protests. Each mule in line responds either kicking the mule nearest, or rearing and tangling themselves in a web leaving them immobile, facing all directions at once, their necks wrapped over each other's backs. The wranglers sort them and the procession halts. The slaves face the breeze. Their impassive gaze moving along the horizon and back, their field of vision expanding with each pass until what they see is not through their eyes.

As though the beasts have discovered snakes beneath their hooves, they squeal in unison, leaping into the air spinning and stumbling. Three break clear and sprint awkwardly east. One's balance fails against its heavy load and topples on its side, rolls and stands stupidly until it begins to backtrack along the trail. The others are run down by the caballeros. Some order is restored, but the more prescient beasts must be beaten. Meanwhile riders from the garrison cross their legs over their mount's backs and await the order to move on.

The slaves are statues. Two horses scream. The male slaves glance at one another and begin praying for a puma or grizzly to descend on them, freeing those who can escape into the hills beyond. The priest whispers questions betraying his fear. The questions are ignored. All eyes search the horizon upwind. Hearts can be seen pounding beneath ribs, horses lower their bellies, their eyes wide white and wild. The hooded slaves stand resigned and motionless as though frozen in an icy wind.

The sun rides the crests to the west, blazing the rolling rims, fighting in a golden fury igniting the sky above the hills.

The beast sees dark forms in the distance and hears the pandemonium of the mules and screaming horses. It charges. Each stride shivers giant muscles under silver-tipped fur. The grizzly groans in a series that could almost sound as though it were urging itself on, if it were not so apparent that nothing represents opposition. A shot cracks. The grizzly ignores it. Three more shots ring out. The garrison forms a half-circle rotating in a wide arch, their muskets firing with the grizzly still out of range. Several riders remove their shirts and balancing under their horses' neck, blindfold their mounts. A wrangler distributes long pikes tipped in a pointing steel finger and thumb. Two horses spring into the air, their riders clinging to their backs.

The churchman yanks the tethers of the girls, losing his grip on one. She senses the slack and immediately disappears into the grass beside the trail. The tether vanishes behind her like a lizard's tail. The other captive snaps side to side against her ever shortening leash. He grabs her by her hair and lifts her cleanly into the air securing her over his mount, his reins in one hand and the other gripped in a claw on the back of her neck.

The beast towers on hind legs rocking left to right surveying the pack train. A shot is followed by another and the bear spins to one side and charges again reaching a mule, ripping its haunches and pulling it off its feet. A paw clubs the side of its head breaking its skull. The mule drops flat. Two shots thunk into the bear's hide. Enraged, it charges past a hooded slave and bowls over a horse. Its rider runs to the side of a companero whose horse rears and throws its own rider clinging for life to the reins. He is stomped beneath his mount's hooves. The rider afoot stands behind several mounted soldiers who struggle to reload. The grizzly is hugging an old slave to his chest, biting her scalp. He tosses her aside. Now lowering its head, gouging her with rapid bites on her face and neck. A shot stings the grizzly on one side. The beast looks for an instant, curious as the ridges over his shoulder bow and swell and his neck lurches forward until it bellows a sound more horrible than those already echoing in the valley around them.

A mule regains its feet, its forelegs buckle, it falls on its face. The slaves scatter in a tangle of falling children. The garrison spurs their terrified horses in a starburst from the center of the mayhem, wheels them around and in the near distance reload their muskets.

The priest and commander are kicking the ribs of their mounts purchasing several yards from the grizzly turning in a slow circle and charging indiscriminately into mules, and slaves. The circle widens around the beast and lariats spin in the air above him. A salvo of musket shot thud into his back. He immediately charges the smoking barrels and the men in panic behind them. A horse falls knocking a second rider to the ground. The rider hobbled by a broken ankle is caught in a sudden surge and slapped to the dust. The grizzly windmills his claws through the rider's stomach and chest, then leaves him in spasms. The bear lumbers toward a knot of wranglers, a lariat falls over its crimson head wet with the blood of its of his victims and his own wounds, yet appearing oblivious to self-preservation. The grizzly runs in a tight circle around the rider. The rider's rope tangles over his shoulder and wraps around his waist. He is pulled to the ground and trails the path of the grizzly as it swats the air charging the nearest enemy. The grizzly retraces its path and finds the rider struggling on his back, kicking the dust beneath him and screaming for God to save him. God does not save him.

The procession moves on, less six slaves, dead or escaped, three riders dead, two horses and one mule dead. The party moves down the trail for four miles under flickering torches before it builds a base camp around a fire as a chill sets in on the night. A large stake is pounded into the ground just outside of the firelight. Two wounded slaves are left as bait, bound and bleeding. The others are placed in a tighter ring of three or four at intervals which form a large circle around the horses. Between the slaves and the horses, the garrison and wranglers sit talking quietly before their small fires, their muskets in their hands. The churchmen sleep nearest the large fire; slaves are brought for warmth in the night.

August Tenth, two hundred and three years later is again, hot. In less time than it has taken to dream, the rutted trail has become a highway of eight concrete lanes. The hot valley is toxic, mixing with sunlight and acrid breezes collecting over the endless malls, furniture warehouses, fast food troughs, burger franchises, a race track, an airport, all within a brown horizon rising, swirling, then raining silently over the valley floor.

Shasta stands white to the north. Jet trails crucifix the sky above the cold white peak, conquering and reducing geology until it is a dead language and what is heard, but not understood, is the skyward hiss of the out-of-time passing of those strapped-in and aloft. Everything below a din of meaningless dramas, screeching, imploring, justifying, excusing and deceiving.

The low afternoon sun glares off thousands of car windows; drivers go blind. Panicked arms wave before burning eyes. Lane changes, accelerations, brakes tossing drivers at their windshields. Grim, gray faces, spruced up in latest style of goatee, Shanghai girls, the inevitable business suits, baseball caps, suburban moms, junkies, professors—vapid, empty, and alone behind their wheels. Jaws clamped tight in end-of-millennia psychosis. Each face and utterance cloned from an image provided by profiteers mindless of the penalty for robbing souls. Liars beyond not telling the truth. Oracles reaching below the belt, into the viscera and yanking the same blood and guts out for those seated and processed to see, to understand, to nod their heads in acceptance of their own fate at eighty miles an hour. They glare in Eddie's rearview mirror, their insolent wrist riding the steering wheel, their faces mouthing obscenities.

Like that Mazda cutting in front of the green Volkswagen bus.

Automatic. Precise. Mindless. One of the zealots behind the wheel, high as God, stamping to the radio bass line, fighting to gain a foot on a slow Volkswagen bus containing a family returning from a camping trip. Dad, balding and wearing his 49er's hat. His wife is in the backseat with their daughter's baby, the younger kids and his ancient sleeping father. His mother sits beside him, a live-wire although withered by living eight decades, chattering along with slow stories of her childhood in Dublin.

The Mazda hits its brakes.

Dad panics. Tires slide. The bus noses over, hits the highway and bounces high, its doors ajar and twisting in the air, falling over the divider and onto coming traffic. The old woman loses her last breath on first impact. From then she is an amazed participant in a ten-car- pile-up one hundred miles north of San Juan Bautista. Her thoughts fade from the exact and blur into riddles and clues. Sifting her life's final magnificent epiphanies. Her vision dims while dying images run like ghosts through her memory. A church. Two shadows running. A graveyard. The stairs to a funeral home. A man in her bed. Her body feels inflated, light, amniotic, swimming in the dark. Her pain is real, and as it is her last pain, she finds the power to transcend it and observe it all floating high above it. Her fingers splayed, pressed on hard transparency, cold and then shattering into a thousand cracks. Her family having to fend, this time, for themselves.

What appears to be a fastball coming over the center divider is a baby shoe careening off Eddie's windshield. The green Volkswagen bus follows, end-over-ending nine feet in the air. Inside an old woman flies weightless her fingers splayed against her window.

The baby shoe shoots over the sunroof.

Fighting the steering wheel everything is falling silent. Slow. Motion. A trumpet peals high over exploding gas tanks and collisions like mini-bombs cascade in spinning circles, metal eggshells collapse and occupants flail in flames slowing in stunning crunches hissing coolant and smoking tires.

Surviving it. Skidding and braking-then-flooring-the-pedal. Nudged and bumped, hit-but-not-hard-and-then-skidding-again with French horns heralding the state of grace it takes to still be alive here. When Eddie finds his voice, it is praying between his gritted teeth for the chance to remain, alive-here-and-for-tomorrow-to-be-here-again.

This strange internal music drowning out the clutter of television commercials, film soundtracks, thumping radio. This din normally blurs his instinct, robs him blind, leaves him sunstroked in a windstorm swirling amongst the debris of this inane culture, all the while skidding over the bones of entire tribes he comes alive, immune for a moment.

Eddie's front tire wobbles and blows, slapping until the rim plows a trail of sparks against the concrete. He's fishtailing, his brakes lock, his tires squeal. People around him howl.

A half mile away, Eddie knows a fifth grade teacher is standing on a school playground noticing grey clouds rising from the direction of the freeway. His windshield shatters.

To his left, a hipster in a Galaxy is rocking past on two wheels. The driver's face is contorted and snow white, his mouth is wide open and he is silent, his eyes are rolling. He pulls to the far lane untouched, sliding along the bumper wall catching the cyclone fence with his rear fender, peeling grey wire diamonds off their posts until it trails him like a thrashing eel.

It all begins to slow. It stops. The Volkswagen slides past on its side spraying sparks. A terrified cartoon spins wildly past, centripetal force pushing him over his seat, his jacket climbs his neck, white cuffs rise to his elbow. He slams into an empty station wagon, its radio playing a gospel choir at full volume, rhythm exploding in clapping hands applauding God's will being done. His head smashes against the dashboard, face spraying mucus and blood, his neck snapping back in forth in time with those ecstatic heavenly wails.

Eddie's car rights itself. He wobbles a few hundred yards and pulls into the emergency lane. A woman with a baby in a car seat pulls in behind him crying hysterically. Sirens wail from someplace. Another car pulls over, a middle-aged man stares straight ahead, paramedics will have to pry his fingers from the steering wheel. Eddie walks back through the chaos and sees a yellow dress fluttering like a butterfly and a family crying beside her.

The sun sets beyond circling lights and crackling radios. The night falls with a line of traffic stretching over the rolling horizon for miles, headlights blazing like torches along a king's highway.

Finally arriving at his apartment at 16th and Dolores, Eddie can't shake the sense that the old woman has not finished yet, or has not finished with him. He turns the key of his empty apartment finding yesterday's heartbreaking weeks of abandonment foreign, from a different world. If she loves him, she should have him. The guy is a mindless lowlife, a simpering whiner. Snaking into a friendship, then moving on her.

You'd have to kill the guy for it to complete itself and she must not be worth it. Or it would be done already. But it lingers on.

But inexplicably Eddie is filled with the desire to live. Fueled with a rage to get back into life and find what is there for him. Like a choral climb inside his head. Feeling like that and imbuing everything with a fresh sense of anticipation. Such a stunning change from black mean hate. To this sense of relief as those prayers he does not remember saying are being answered anyway. In just a matter of hours. He thinks about the old woman—she spins in the air above him again.

The world opens up. The travel section jumps at him from the coffee table. Laughable to rehash the split, the tears, her beauty, weighing the chance she might come back.

Face it, the best sex was behind you anyhow, all that remained was habit. Eddie, she lied to you anyway. Your appreciation of her beauty was, after all, narcissistic, some tribal resemblance, some link to auburn hair, blue-eyed, Irish fantasy. Your kind. Blood lines or something. Weird how simple it is when its power is removed.

In an hour, music reappears in Eddie's apartment. Three hours later, the floor is slick with album sleeves—he's drunk, stoned. It's time for a walk.

Outside. The clear air carries distant sounds. Echoing parts of conversations, cars clearing intersections, dogs on tinkling leashes. A drunken shout. Breaking glass. Eddie forgot his jacket and the fog is streaming over twin peaks. A mist descending. Past the mission cemetery, all the McNamara headstones. Duggan's. Kennedy's. O'Brien's. Eddie lays on his couch. The glass. Her old face behind the glass. Shattering. Asleep. Her fluttering dress in the highway. The gurney, the disconsolate son, the confused grandchildren.

Just sixty years ago someone else was holding absolute possession of her body, and certain that much of her mind, and parts of her soul were also his to keep in what was becoming an eternity. Aroused beyond what he thought possible, he gave himself away. He saw her face more beautiful, and then almost horrible, in her release of love.

What he was thinking was wrong, what he felt was misleading, what he hoped for was futile. She wasn't on the bed with him, not really before him, laying loose and lost within the close, hot room. It was her sweat and her ragged breathing, her muttered sputters. The nails in his back were hers. But she was not there. Her senses were within her mind; her eyes saw nothing open or closed. She was gone and didn't know how she had done it. He never guessed the intensity he felt within her was not sourced in her body, but in her complete absence. She was betraying him. She violated him further, taking him into a chamber he would see just once, an ancient treachery coming over her like an echo, unwanted, undeniable. Coming over him like a sunset on a distant horizon. A sight which at that moment struck him as indescribably beautiful, although strangely familiar.

In the next moment he fell into a panic, sensing exactly what the problem was, and unable to contain his accusation. She wiping tears off her face; her lips pulled tight over her teeth. Her tentative denial driving him crazy.

She turned her face to the wall as he raved in the hallway. She saw thousands of women choosing black, pleading with the Virgin for relief, finding a faint recognition and communion in her downward gaze.

Dawn at 16th and Dolores. A wagon rattles along the corner, horses tired and rocking voluptuously, hips swaying, halters creaking. Four longshoremen jostle easily in the wagon bed, smoking and complaining. Two automobiles compete for the right of way. The intersection clears into a right angle of fate timed with a closing alley bar and the end of a late night card game. The two men recognize the identity of the other. They stride the gray walkway with an increasing pace, each in the path of the other, as though hurrying to pray beyond the marble stairs of the towering Mission San Francisco de Assisi, turning harsh in the reddish light above them.

One of the turning points in violence is in fear's pause, providing second thought's first grab at irresolution, provoking the leap into action by the foolishly brave. A hand reaches into a jacket and removes a fishing knife. A man stoops and snatches a beer bottle, cracking it on a stone curb.

The first swipe with the knife misses. The fist juts under his swing and glass rakes deep along his wrist and over the forearm, torn veins gushing and splashing. The bleeding man steps back, amazed at the damage. His bellow echoes off the plaster walls above him. The bottle gashes him again, tearing a red belt around his waist. He snatches the knife clattering along the ground and moves into the man who's standing with his head tilted as though he were drawing a conclusion. The knife drives into his thigh and would have run up into the groin if they hadn't slipped, the blade glinting downward leaving a line to knee. The pant leg changes color. If they didn't know one of them would be dead at first, they knew it now.

They circle each other, shuffling and scraping. Eyes fixed with cold purpose and forlorn sadness at the result of it all gone hopelessly out of hand. They spit in muttered taunts. They levitate above a half-dressed crowd standing in shafts of sunlight, unable to take their eyes off this passion making death entirely tangible before them. The spectators protest, then reconcile. Eyes dart from one to the other wondering who will stop it, until they realize they do not want it stopped. The figures flail in the muck until one dies and one lives. The mute crowd turns away, their thrilled faces glancing back, their shame driving them home. A voice calls in protest, a choir responds in kind. The crowd vanishes.

A man lying face up twitches for twenty minutes as shock and blood loss lift his ghost. The other stands for a moment over him, then walks four blocks to find an empty horse stall at his brother's livery and collapses. His arm is amputated ten days later at the shoulder. Convicted of murder a month after that. No chance for parole.

She moved out of town to a place in the outskirts of Shasta, married a milkman. Had four kids. Never had a love again that came close to either man. Never wrote the prisoner. Visited the grave every year, until she turned eighty-two and died in a ten car inferno. Never lost her Irish accent.

SUIT OF LIGHTS

The bull's stride explodes, spewing chunks off the arena floor. The sand shakes beneath your feet in rhythmic power. He squints you into focus beneath ten-inch horns.

You only have five seconds—three to find the position, two to plant the feet. The beast blasts past, leaving salt, piss, snot and blood over your face.

Your rivals hope for the worst. She waits at home, to give you what you need to stay alive.

SOUTH

Crickets outside. Dew on the grass. Dogs asleep. Dawn coming.

Walking down the stairs into the foundry of his dreams. Figures shimmer in the heat, staring at him—old men, black and sweating, heroic Rivera renderings. WPA posters come to life. Huge Soviet women with thick-soled boots, bare-breasted, laboring, surrounded with flames, pausing momentarily, leaning on the handles of their shovels, watching Eddie dreaming of them.

A woman is doused. She steams and draws an artifact from the fire, passing it to a crippled man who fixes it on an anvil with a series of deft and practiced maneuvers in a dance. His tongs ring like bells as the women's hammers clang, waking him in full adrenaline spasms.

The radio alarm gives news of thunderstorms and murder. Eddie's middle age moves part by part. The bed springs creak. His feet hit the floor; he stands up unsure of his balance. Dizzy and nauseous, he totters to the bathroom. His face in the mirror looks like an astronaut breaking through gravity's pull.

He splashes his face—eyes tired and empty.

The radio drones on. Washington is moving to Salem. Maniacs are devouring children. Playmates are beating each other to death. Mothers are tossing their newborns off bridges. Racism and misogyny are holding hands in the back of the hall.

Someone's body is whomping against the wall. He waits until he is sure no one has yelled for help.

The newspaper hits the front porch. Chronicles of the worst the city can offer, huddled in blankets in doorways, breathing in the sidewalks littered with condoms, tubercular oysters, piss, blood, grease and shit. Old men flapping in their jackets to keep from freezing to death. Enraged youth menace the street looking for the chance to prove that they really don't give a fuck about anything, no more than anything cares about them, which is, let's face it, not at all.

Eddie grimaces in the mirror and begins to examine his teeth. A clap of thunder rolls over the house.

Pausing, rubbing the warm terry cloth under his balls, he stands there in vapor, naked and beginning to sweat. Stunned by a memory beginning to take shape, he waits.

A throbbing BMW filled with junior high warriors shakes the bathroom walls—blunts, a chorus of psychotic lyrics, fingers on the trigger, eyes cold for anyone outside their set.

Maybe the Vikings were right. Maybe you want to die in battle because you know every succeeding battle is worse. If we're heading toward Armageddon anyway, why not get it over with?

Eddie had his chance. The roar of automatic fire drowned in the whomping blades above him. Hugging his weapon, burping rounds at anything moving. Buffaloes collapsing where they stand, peasant kids splattering, grandmas face down, shreds of vegetation spinning in the air. 'Cause he is getting his ass back to the world.

Getting dressed, changing the radio's channel, hearing the old tunes again. All of them so unbelievably sad. He believed in magic. He was ready for life.

Looking through his drawer for socks that match, he recalls the bitter November in 1969. Mascots blowing over the border into California all night long, landing on high schools, over taco stands, affixing themselves as logos on business cards—Matadors... Aztecs... Toros.

A long time ago. Nineteen years old, crossing into Mexico with his girlfriend Diane and her family. Heading down to the Tecate mountains to meet three other families for a weekend of desert camping, drinking and card playing. Bouncing over dirt roads on a black moonless night. Mom and Dad in the front seat, his hand on the inside of Diane's leg, her little brother sleeping on Eddie's shoulder. Dad pulls over to let Mom drive because he started drinking before they left San Diego.

He has a funny feeling about this. It started back on the paved road before they hit the switchbacks climbing the mountains behind Tijuana. The old man squealing tires on each turn, past a yellow sign that reads *Peligroso*. He answered her little brother's question.

"It means dangerous."

The words squashed flat in the low roof of the station wagon, disappearing with the engine noise. The air smells sweet with gin, tonic and hair spray. He cracks the window. Cold air rushes in.

They set up camp. Gathering wood for the fire falls to Eddie.

High desert holds time still. Crumbled granite crunches under each step further into the dark. Ghosts appear and transform him, sprinkling coats of dust from sage and manzanita. He's becoming indigenous. He hears them breathing. The branches shake above him. Their ankle bells stamp in the dark.

They're praying in other words, timed with the thud of the desert's pulse, exorcising his civilization, putting him in harmony with the moonless night and its cold November wind.

Stumbling the armload back to camp, trying to make out the whispers around him. The desert observing the invaders, watching the bumbling strangers bustling in the shadows. He can hear their voices shaking with fear. The wind picks up and turns him back toward camp.

There should be three more families meeting them out here. It's too dangerous to be isolated this deep in fugitive bandit territory. There's no sign of anyone. No bleary toasts, no hearty camper greetings, no snapping cards. One family in the middle of the mountains, just asking for it.

Diane's father is gently forcing another gin and tonic on his wife, domestic style.

"Here, honey."

She is fighting for the focus of her husband through his Bombay and Schweppes blur. He has an office girl under his desk. She has two kids and a drunk whom she never takes her eyes from—a high school sweetheart, the one and only love of her life. Her self-definition as wife and mother, the only goals of her life, coming down around her shoulders with lying phone messages, missed meals and sexless nights. Eddie hears her pleading, "John, look at me," in everything she does. A blanket for him, another drink, hushing the kids, laughing at his jokes, taking his mumbling bullshit seriously.

Eddie drops the firewood and escapes toward the brush. Diane, in the later stages of Juliet, raw and combustible, intercepts him.

It's in her expression. She's scared. She holds him in her arms in a grip that is not affectionate, more than sexual. It's a need and it comes from fear. She tries to disguise it with a long kiss. When it doesn't work, she disappears.

The trail boss is drunk. Sloppy, tongue out of synch, "Thaaaa, thaa, thaaa." Body weaving. He's becoming aware that his family is alone. He needs another drink.

Eddie thinks he hears something. His face turns up to the sky. It is cold, clear, moonless. Stars. A canopy strewn above. He revolves; the silver dots spin.

He stops, having unconsciously determined the hour of the day in Vietnam, wondering what is happening over there. Wondering what he would do. He is fixed dead center in the draft board's crosshairs. Appealing... being denied... appealing again... being denied again. First appealing as a conscientious objector. Interviewed by seven adults seated at a gleaming wooden table. The women tight-lipped, layered in make-up, beehive hair with pencils sticking out. The men in JC Penney suits and run-over shoes. Every face white and lined with suffering.

Appeal denied in the mail. Report for induction the next week. Appeal the appeal. Same seven criminals hardened in the last few weeks by statistics of casualties, enraged by Life Magazine's page after page of soldiers killed in one week's issue. Schoolboys in helmets, pointing their fingers.

"Son, no one wants war... least of all us."

Stated clearly that he will not carry a weapon, will not shoot anyone. Will be a medic. The seven jumped in their chairs. Saying he understands that under Geneva's rules, aid can be given to the men, women and children of the farming class in Vietnam, which the government seems to see as the enemy.

The second appeal is now a shouting match. Eddie hot, pounding the table. The chairs flying back as the men take their feet. The women shocked. Security summoned.

"Bullshit. You'll be inducted. You will serve in the US Army and you will do what ever they demand of you."

"I'll punch the first guy who gives me an order and keep punching..."

"Your way to prison."

Quiet.

"Listen here, son. When you fuck with the Army, you ain't with a virgin."

She says this coughing as she lights up another cigarette, which by the time she says "virgin," is lit and bouncing between her lips.

"Put you in a Negro barracks and you'll be the best soldier in Fort Ord. Or you'll be the most pathetic little doggie you ever saw."

"Fuck you."

Appeal denied.

Stumbling over a root and staggering to keep his balance with his armload of branches, Eddie thinks of his friends in boot camp and shudders.

A new vision in the dark—the smell of shining silver coyote, the snap of a branch with the percussive pop under his boot. Land mines, schoolmates, shrapnel. Another world, where there is war. Where there are people, there are wars. Not here, not now. Arguing with himself in the dark. The prelude to prayer.

Moving into the light of camp. Dropping the firewood. Going to the station wagon, waving off the voices saying, "Finally." Turning off the headlights, starting the car. Answering, "Nowhere," when Dad slurs an inquiry about where the hell ya been. Watching his face, his eyes beyond focus. Leaving the engine running. Back to the pile of firewood, the little boy placing hardwood from home over the brush. As you douse the pile with lighter fluid, you apologize to those elements who watch you out there. *Whoosh.* Warmth coming soon, sparks flying already, flickering light over shadows. Animation of imagined giants and specters standing on the edge of firelight and fifty miles of desert. Deadly silence.

"Don't waste gas."

He's falling into a chair he has dragged too close to the fire.

"Sorry."

You turn off the engine. Hoping the generator recharged the battery enough to start the wagon again.

Coming back to the fire, watching faces staring into flames. Diane sharing her parka with her brother, rocking back and forth in a crouch before it. Her mother turning to rub her round ass over the flames. Hands cupping bottom for an instant, curving up and over, down and cupping again, more pressure. Unconscious shift widening her stance. *Peligroso.*

A truck gears down in the black valley, about the point where the asphalt road turns to dirt. Diane's head turns down toward the valley. Her mother steps back from the fire.

"Must be the Reynolds coming."

Relief in her voice. The release of tension drops the drunk deeper into his chair. Something tells Eddie the muffler is too loud.

Knotting his forehead in a series of fleshy question marks, his eyes bugged in disbelief. One eyebrow climbing, he signals Diane to follow him. She does. She tries to speak. His finger presses her lips. They listen in silence. The muffler is too loud.

"Diane, go back to camp. That's not the Reynolds down there, it's someone else. I think... We... Diane listen to me."

His arms unwrap hers from around his chest, his tone becomes firm, absolutely condescending. A movie cowboy telling the little lady to get in the wagon. There seems to be no other way to communicate but through these ridiculously inadequate means. This is no time to struggle with the new vocabulary they've tried to teach each other.

"Diane, I said go back to camp. I'll be there in a minute."

She gives Eddie a look that chips a part of what they hope for away. She takes his patronizing culture with her back to camp, strides stamping, pounding out her fear of not quite knowing why she is so offended.

Every breeze, the cold of the night, the scratch of the brush, the crunch under his boots, the dryness of his lips—all combine to alarm him. Fear engulfs Eddie whole. An isolated family in the Tecate mountains, a drunken father, a dependent wife, two children snared in the convention of family hierarchy and an outsider boyfriend as a wild card. And something looming. Something real bad. His spine jumps as though he'd fallen in ice. His heart pounds wondering if the fear that is coming is really that far out of his up-to-now known experience. *If this is the first wave, then shit, this is more than I can handle. I'll fall apart.* The ground opens under his feet. He feels like he is doing a very slow back flip. His head is jabbering; the voice inside is screaming.

"*Hide. They'll never find you. But they'll find Diane and the rest of them.*"

Recon. That's what you've heard it called. See them before they see you. Who? How many? Other campers coincidentally out here in the high desert mountains late on a November night? Not likely. Say the word. Go ahead. Banditos.

War coming here? Violence is a living, breathing being stalking the world, bearing down on those in the path and tearing them to pieces. Eddie's best friend is on the other side of the world, coming in from the jungle. His letter is in Eddie's pocket. Five Hueys in, two Hueys out the first day in Vietnam. Three helicopters of teenagers in uniform blown to splatters and flames before they had time enough to... do what? Says there are things you do that you know you'll never forgive. Feels like everything he does is part of a ritual. One that keeps playing out in different places with different languages all over the world. A black mass casting magic on everything. And it must, because it creeps in through the skin as far away as these lonely mountains in Mexico.

Eddie swings from bush to bush, grabbing branches, slowing his descent. Fear rising in unpredictable waves, engulfing him, stealing his breath. The distance from the known, the familiar and the recognizable is immense. A sense of the convergence with faceless powers turning the corner, planning to take his life. The sense of what it is to be, and what it is we have by just being alive. Win or die. The last, most horrible and intimate human encounter. Dying at the hands of another. The final disgrace.

The muffler is silent. Eddie hears more in the next seconds than he has heard in his life. The wind, branches snagging his jacket, rustling in the distance, and voices—males speaking Spanish... coming this way. He turns and runs uphill silently.

Is this what makes you whole? Is this how you reach your entirety? Are you alive now?

Layers of fatigue bring new layers of pain, ushering in new levels of himself in the ascent to camp. Balance requires additional strength; noise will bring disaster. Control the breathing, gasps that whisper. Stop at the sight of the campfire. Breathe deeply. Do not make them panic. They're still moving in pretend comfort, still acting for what they each hope passes for normal.

Diane's mother's face is shocked. Eddie demands that she keep her control. One look combined with a silent flick of Eddie's fingers is all it takes. Her eyes lock on him for the next move. He heads for the station wagon, his eyes searching for the shotgun. She moves toward the door, opens it as he crosses the camp. Diane's brother is asking an innocent question about scorpions and winter and sleeping bags.

"Not in winter, under rocks."

He reaches the open door. Her fingers shake as she points to the blanket she has yanked aside, the cloth case. It weighs nothing as the zipper is yanked down and all eyes in camp look up. The barrel slides into view. Eddie's hand pats down the case looking.

"Julie, where are the shells?"

Never used her name before.

"Glove compartment. What is it?"

"Nothing I hope. A truck stopped down the hill. Men are coming this way."

Her mouth opens and closes, her eyes see something grim.

"John, I..."

Her voice is hard, demanding. She looks over at the man in the chair balancing a weaving glass toward his lips, eyes half shut.

"John, we have to start packing..." Her eyes look to Diane, who has frozen, hearing the sound in her voice and watching Eddie load the shotgun.

Diane is immediately by her brother's side. He's aware that his child's body is unprepared for what may be coming—what is coming. Eddie's body grows rigid in determination, his shoulders square, his feet are no longer touching the ground. He clears his throat.

"John..."

His name.

"John..." His voice is changed. "We better get out of here." Eddie slides another shell into the chamber.

"John, please."

Julie's voice hits an upper register near panic. She cuts herself off and freezes her face into place. Her heart drops down down down, spiraling down in one more utterance.

"Dammit John!"

Diane and her brother are moving toward the car. John is beginning to sense something and gathers his balance for the effort to get to his feet. The moment stops.

"*Buenos noches.*"

Eddie is addressing the ghosts at the edge of the camp light.

A man walks into the flickering light. His rifle glints in the red flame. Dusty boots, baggy pants. Down jacket. Cowboy hat. Eyes deep in burned brown face.

"*Buenos noches.*"

His words signal the steps into light of two companions—one probably a brother with missing fingers on one hand, the other much smaller with a belt buckle catching light. They're drunk.

Eddie steps away from the family. The shotgun in his hands points exactly to the middle of the distance between him and the man who spoke. The man smiles a mirthless grin. His eyes have scanned everything. He sees nothing to stop him. His companions fan out into a semicircle taking control of half of the camp. Three rifles. Three men. One shotgun. One boy. One man drunk in a chair, jumping to his feet, catching his balance and walking toward Eddie, his hand out for the gun.

They'll probably open fire when he hands it to him.

"Eddie, give me the gun."

"*Que quires?*"

Eddie stares at the man who's watching Diane and running his eyes over Julie. The companions move three easy steps closer.

John's voice is snarling.

"Give me the gun."

Eddie pumps the action. The sound is answered by the cocking of the rifles.

"*Que pasa?*" demands the voice across the fire.

"*Nada, pero no quiero...*"

In the exchange of these words is the last chance to give the gun to John before he tries to grab it.

John has the gun. Eddie is disarmed. The men are nearly laughing in his face. There is nothing to do but to try to act as though this situation is no cause for alarm. An attempt at normalcy. Disarm the situation, make the world around him consistent with his own helplessness under the guns.

Eddie walks to the beer cooler.

"*Quien quire una cerveza?*"

There is a light chuckle from the man furthest to his right. He steps forward. During his strides, his rifle points at Eddie's balls. As he reaches him, it slowly lowers to the space between his feet. He knows Eddie felt the threat. Eddie hands him a beer.

"*Gracias.*" Big smile.

Diane and her brother are beside the station wagon. The man

cracking the beer watches her with something going on in his head. She will suck his dick. The boy will suck his dick. The boy will take it up the ass. She will suck her brother's dick. The mother will scream and cry. Nobody will hear her. Their drunken father will go out of his mind. His smile rests on Eddie's face. His eyebrow raises wondering what Eddie will do. He turns away, ahead of Eddie. He's been there before. He can almost see the twisted bodies. He sees strangers finding them days later.

The circle has closed; the men can almost touch each other. The companions never remain completely still. The first man reaches out for the shotgun, gesturing with his own rifle that he would like to trade them.

John hesitates. The thought races through his mind that he can parlay this into some sort of male ritual. His companion walks to the cooler and takes two beers, stuffs one into a jacket pocket. He sucks the other one down in three long gulps. John is offended. He wants to assert himself. He weighs his pride against his fear; the scales tip. He loses what is left of his confidence. He notices a powerful need for a drink press in on his throat.

David's voice is barely out before Diane has slapped her hand over his mouth.

"Dad, don't give him the gun."

John comes to his senses. He begins to think about shooting his way out. The barrel moves half an inch toward the man who stands grinning, his own rifle held away from him, his hand on the barrel half a foot from the trigger. John is giving his thoughts away. The man scowls hard. John shakes. His face reddens to a lobster, veins pound over his forehead.

"*Quires mas cerveza?*"

No response. Eddie's voice gives away nothing. His own tone encourages him. He hasn't gotten on his knees in this strange new world yet.

"*No? Entonces...*"

He hunches over the cooler, grabs the side handles and begins to walk it to the station wagon.

The four men don't move. The man who offered the gun exchange squats down on his haunches.

"*Amigo. Una mas, por favor.*"

Eddie puts down the cooler next to the station wagon. He lifts the cooler into the back. Eddie's eyes meet Diane's; she blinks in desperation. Eddie tries to smile, but his lips only grimace.

Eddie walks, two beers in hand, across the campfire, directly to the man rising from his squat and hands him a beer. Eddie raises his beer to the three of them.

"*Salud.*"

He laughs and returns the gesture. Eddie looks him in the eye and says, "*Buenos noches, y adios.*"

Turning his back, grabbing a camp chair and folding it as he reaches the station wagon.

"*Si, adios,*" says the man and he begins to move backward out of the campfire light. His companions leave with him.

In the dark, one of the men begins whistling. The three of them walk loudly, two speaking with animation and laughter in sentences no one can make out. The sounds fade.

Eddie gives Diane and David orders. The sound of it is strange; the energy behind it is both affectionate and absolutely final.

"Lay down on the floor in the back seat. Don't move. Don't look up. Don't do anything no matter what you hear."

Eddie senses that he may never say another thing to them. Eddie leaves before they can think of it.

The truck starts up. The muffler begins to grumble down the hill.

"We have to pack. We have to get out of here."

Julie can talk.

"They're between us and the highway," she realizes out loud. "I don't care. We have to get out of here."

Adrenaline amplifies the gin in John and he fires four shots into the night sky. Exactly the wrong thing to do. Panic on display.

He pulls shells out of the box and tries to cram them into the cylinder.

"John... Stop it! Stop it! Stop it!"

She's hysterical.

He's dropping shells on the ground and managing to fire off four more rounds into the surrounding brush.

A shot from down the mountain side. Three echoes and the truck's gears winding higher.

"Julie, where's the keys?"

She pounds her pockets. Eddie runs to the driver's door, jerks it open. No keys in the ignition. She's screaming.

"Where's the goddamn keys?"

He's muttering. The shotgun's jammed.

The truck stops.

"Ok, Julie..." A hard sentence comes out of Eddie's mouth. "They're coming back."

His voice sounds deadened and flat. John is reduced to near convulsions, his hands shaking, the gun falling. He picks it up. Dirt fills the jammed chamber.

Two more shots echo from below, louder and closer. Eddie runs to the back of the station wagon, yanks out the cooler, runs to the fire and douses it in a hiss of smoke. He kicks the embers of the wet pile.

John is defeated. The gun is hopelessly jammed and he's too drunk to solve it. He slumps, his shoulders drop, his head is down. He's thinking about himself, what he's done, where he is, what he is. He can't move. He's about to cry.

Julie is moving in silence. She frisks her husband, going through his pockets. No keys.

Eddie is suddenly warm. He sways inside, his soul getting a glimpse of everything. Nothing can reach him. A weight so dense he can't be moved. The message the desert whispered to him in what seems like a lifetime ago is the closest thing to love he's ever felt.

"*I'll already be dead before I see anything happen to them.*"

He grabs the camp shovel, its blade folded down, the pick sticking out at a right angle. He tightens the blade down, twisting the hand screw on the short handle. He walks out into the brush, listening for their steps. He crouches beside their path.

He waits, hearing their footsteps crashing through brush below. Eddie decides to use the edge of the shovel blade. The pick might get stuck in the bones of their faces.

WHEN RELATIONSHIPS GO BAD

Eddie's mind has become a prisoner. The battle for his soul was lost before his age had two digits. The remainder of his life becomes an anguished search. In the dark. In strange terrain.

It is understandable that he would eventually lock himself up, hiding from these cities filled with cannibals, like vultures, up to their necks in the chest cavities of the fallen dead, their spasms twitching to music they try to call their own. Obscene gyrations and thrusts in doorways and on street corners. Everyone thinking they're on time, bopping to the rhythm, nodding with the bass, mouthing the words, thinking that's enough to own it, to have made it, to be it. On hands and knees, the vultures grin down on your face and shake hands before turning you over.

Eddie seems safe inside himself. A red stain rings the walls of his prison cell. His fingers bleed as high as he can reach. I have been made to understand that he will forever be denied parole. So he wrestles around in there with his fear one minute and the guilt for dirty fighting the next. I don't see any way out. They see right through him. You probably have a better story than his. They'll probably believe you. You get along better with the others anyway.

I still get time in the yard. They let me out on cold days. I shiver in the wind like an ice carving. Eyes are grey and sightless; cannibals walk past me without comment. I just stand here... waiting. Feeling myself going numb, until the season changes and a smell comes from me that fills the air with this year's progression toward complete rot. Then feeling returns, and each nerve ending screams. The impulse is to go north to the ice, to freeze and be numb again.

But they smile, encircling my bent shoulders in their arms, pushing the plate in my direction, testing the bath water, boiling the tea, making the bed, setting the alarm. Locking the door quietly, telling me they'll come back. In warm sleep, the body gains strength and wakes. I hear the key in the door. Their faces peer at me, patient and infinitely understanding like nuns above reproach. Vicious in their tolerance, and spiteful in their understanding. Thinking I don't recognize this love as something feeding itself on what there is to hate in me.

I walk outside. Hands in my pockets, head down, walking and thinking, walking and wondering. I witness an underdog. I hear insults following him down the street. I wonder about Eddie. How he's doing. Is he still making it worse for himself?

In a park, I watch in the pale dusk, children abandon each other. That night I make it to the edge of town where the bars and clubs hold the wicked and the chaste, mingling in an unholy and inevitable attraction. I hear the snide, witty condemnation that seems un-armed, and watch it blow a hole right through the innocent person not quite up to understanding the words snaking out of the hipster's broken mouth. Parked cars shine with pre-dawn dew, and in their windows my eyes look a lot more tired. Another loser begs for a quarter to make the bus.

This is a battlefield without honor. It evaporated from the trenches, the camps, under the blaze of Christendom's ground zero.

You don't get a quarter. Please don't make a fool of yourself seeking mercy. Here we kill children as a matter of course.

I keep walking. A dog lifts its tired head and lets it fall back in the dust again, as if it knows there isn't much use in aspiration. The hollow sound of my footsteps blows away with the trash. He jumps and howls in an afterthought behind me.

Then one of you helps the cranky lady off the bus, and a lonely kid hears his name called to him across a barren street. An ancient black gentleman in suit and tie tips his hat, turns the corner and passes me. I hear horns climbing, a warm percussion surrounds me, something genuine happens for an instant in the slightest nod of our heads timed with something we can't understand.

I find it worth living in these simple human gestures, carrying the assurances of shared centuries, the potential for dignity, the promise of something more than the waste around us. The nod of one stranger to another. These singular moments of communion in every church in the world, formalized in the minds of philosophers from every echoing palace throughout time, and failing in every eon.

Wars are fought to retain the nod of one man to another. We call it by other names. We demand allegiance to it—prayer—torture in its name. It has to be disguised, distorted, and defined to fit the need of the commandant. Made into a flag, or symbol, or sentiment fed back to us, to fatten us for the sidewalk. Giving us names and identities so that we can recognize each other. All systems operate to replicate your shadow, to give you company. This single demand of those who rule or who have ever ruled to do this, to duplicate what once was you, is the proof that it takes strangers to dignify the world, to make it safe.

As I near my cell, the reverberation hits the deep keys. I stumble and apologize into my jacket cuff. The door swings open and I reclaim my life, giving the commandant my regrets but I won't be serving chocolate tonight to those educated friends yawning on the living room couch. All of them comfortable, pretending the halls were built for them, that the towers above them aren't dwarfing them, and the dogs outside aren't waiting for a lot more than the scraps no one can really afford to toss in their direction.

A woman is sharpening her feelings for me, grinding her glinting angry woman's broken hearted blade, mouthing incantations. The blade snaps between rib and cartilage. I stagger in circles.

A grass fire burns down the prison farm. The well runs dry. The livestock go mad in the heat and run off. Parasites eventually drive them to blindness. They run in the ashes, tongues swollen, kicking crazily in the air.

We try to be good. We adopt what we associate as good. Grass fires burn down our communities. The wells run dry. We go mad in the heat, killing and running through the night. We go blind. We fight in the ashes. Tongues swollen from repeated lies, we whip ourselves bloody. We move to Salem and the trials begin.

Nobody notices. It's not on the news. All communication becomes complete fiction designed to intimidate. It works like a charm. The Christians win it all and it turns to shit in front of them. Their children begin to revolt. Infections decimate millions, the rest turn to brutal methods of what they see as self-defense. They snap at each other across the dining room table. Spit sputtering in invectives in the disagreement of the moment's entertainment.

It gets quiet for a few hundred years. Small groups of tribesmen begin to communicate, resulting in blood feuds. The night falls.

SEE ME LIKE THIS

A person never knows what they're into until they know what they're up against. I've got an invisible battlefield going these days. Though I can hear the screaming and splattering, the pleading, and the derisive laugh of the conqueror, invisible and present, I find no place to turn.

Pets shriek wherever I put my feet. I wander from corner to corner, room to room, from bed to mirror from challenge to cowering denial, all in a single spinning gray minute. Hating what I am for seeing what I could have been. Loving those who are free of this nausea and disgrace. I can see, but cannot do. I can hear, but I can't see. I know my name, but I never want to say it or hear it.

I contaminate a hundred people a day, all of them thinking I know something. They're right, I do. But the joke is, I learned it twenty years ago and haven't sweated in a moment's labor since. I just lie here with my hands crossed over my chest, my eyes closed, my sleep deep. I hammer myself like a nail deeper into exhaustion.

I see you—hopeful, courageous, naive. Innocent in efforts that will fail you and exalt you before taking your lives down a dark stream where there is no comfort and less air, until your lungs collapse and your eyes bulge.

But until then, you are all peaking, on top of it. Like poker-faced gamblers threatened with ruin. A generation set adrift. A whaling fleet sailing into the coming oblivion. Romantic in the distance, your shadow standing in the prow, revealed in close-up, lashed to the anchor housing. Your conversation interrupted with intermittent seas freezing over you in cold foam.

I hear you stammering around words just audible, the words I also said loud and in whispers, always meaning the same freedom you keep close to your heart.

"Fuck it."

The strain of effort convulsing your blue lips. You are absolutely nonchalant heroes—the very best kind. Your efforts are not wasted, but they are drowned in the seas exploding around you.

Sure, there is something that passes for life, and there is the life you are living. You get energy from the people sensing who you are, and describing and copying for themselves what you are not. When others get you wrong, it doesn't seem to bother you in the least. You seem to have the capacity to say, "It's their problem," and not let it faze you.

I do the whole thing backwards. If someone labels me, or tries to look at me in that perfectly awful, insightful, misunderstanding and self-deprecating way—that need to elevate, that tendency to build up, because we know what follows—I'll find the nearest dog shit to step in, gum to sit on, or horrible belch to burp, like a compulsion. I can't stand for anyone to be more awkward, self-hateful, stupid, or inappropriate than I am. But it's only a defense because with most of them I don't care. Not a bit. In fact, I'm ashamed to admit; the act of fucking with them, confusing them, and making them feel superior to me is my most malicious act. I know for certain that if they tried to track me down, they'd get zero, back to nowhere. So there's my method for dealing with the deserved mistrust and repulsion I feel for the psychological lives of my brothers and sisters: dog shit, gum, and bad air.

It works most of the time. But the problem is dealing with the one percent I find to love. I mean it's nearly suicidal when it comes to those you love, if ninety-nine percent of the time you are in the practice of dodging and distorting yourself. You miss the switch when you're with those you love and the train rolls right past. You begin to lack the skill to make sense to those you care about. You get uncool and self-destructive. You make hurried comments. You say things that mean too much and too little at the same time. You tell a friend not to hold his breath, someone you know never has and never will hold his breath for anything, including toxic fumes.

A person doesn't know what they're into until they know what they're up against. I figured all this out right here at the typewriter. It took me days. I always feel so shitty trying to communicate to anyone I love, long distance or short. I have learned to stand aside and stay quiet most of the time. You know what I'm saying, with you, and those I have and those I will love... Hell, you are the last people I would want to see me like this.

YOU'LL RUIN THAT BOY

My parents left the trailer park behind. For weeks we'd heard about a place called California. A place where a lot more was possible. Oranges. Beaches. Summer all year long. California for us meant moving into a housing tract populated by ex-military families.

Fathers were guards at K-Mart, Fuller Brush salesmen, owner-operators of big rigs, fishermen in the tuna fleet, gardeners, awning salesmen, supers at Lockheed. Or like my father, they were still sailing in fleets around the world, afraid to come home.

In school I made friends with other boys who missed their fathers. Boys who knew they'd see them six or nine months later when the fleet came back to port. We rotated between houses where a man was home, trying to see what they looked like, what they might expect of us.

The Monroes from Texas lived a couple houses down the street. Lyle Monroe became one of those fathers. Lyle always did what he wanted to most of the time. He drank when he wanted. He slept when he felt like it. Got into more women than he had a right to. He was scary, which we as boys interpreted as some organic link to the vindictive, jealous Father in the clouds who for generations had been sending the men in our families to hell. A man of physical strength and nasty disposition who especially despised education and the things that came with it, he broke horses and worked as a prison guard.

He stood over me. His eyes searching my face for the fear I was hiding from him.

"You'll ruin that boy."

I had no idea what he was talking about. What could I do that would ruin his boy? Robert Monroe was beyond ruining. But there are times to keep your mouth shut, and in a canyon alone with Lyle when he'd been drinking was one of them. I was surprised he didn't already know that his boys Robert and Grant were indestructible. The only ruination in their future was whatever they brought down on someone else. But Lyle was in a telling mood, not a hearing one. He stood up straight, almost to his toes. He shook his head and clenched and unclenched his fists. He turned his back to me.

The sweat in his shirt patched between his wide shoulders. He was the kind of man no one could reach, a dangerous mystery to everyone, including his family. His brothers were similar. Lyle was the eldest, each one meaner than the last. The youngest, Boomer, came through town twice a year and slept for the night in the garage. Lyle warned us away, telling us that if we went in there, Boomer would rape us for sure. We peeked under the garage door, watching him laying on the floor masturbating in a drunken stupor. Lyle would always give him two days, then run him off. The two of them in the front yard, bashing on one another's head until Boomer staggered off, screaming threats.

I thought that Lyle was going to walk away, that his comment about my effects on his oldest boy was a passing bit of alcoholic insight, lost and forgotten. He was likely to just start walking, or he might whirl around and slap my face. It had happened before. I waited.

His hands hung like hooks, knuckles thick and callused. He could have been a tall man but he was compressed with a psychic weight which pressed down on his shoulders like Blake's God. He turned slowly; his eyes narrowed with the impulse to hit me. I stood looking up trying to determine the correct response to appease him. That morning, I had knocked his son's front teeth out.

I had my reasons and any of them were sure to make it all worse. I had already been naked in bed with his daughter. And I lusted for his wife.

I didn't really know what having his wife would mean beyond a fascination with her loose curves, her generous lips, the greasy black hair, the deep cleavage of her breasts, the darkened alley between her legs. Her smile and her warm voice. Her quiet ways and her secret rumbling laugh. Her loneliness. There was really nothing I could say.

She ran through my dreams unencumbered with the weight of the guilt she inspired in the daylight hours. Her dark voice speaking a language I could not fathom, but engendered such a need to follow that my waking hours were filled with memories of the sight, smell and sound of her. It was something beyond love and there was no way to tell Lyle that I couldn't help it. It was impossible to explain how it led to the fights I had with his son.

He walked back toward home without saying another word, as though he was stating what was preordained, and there was no point in trying to change it.

I was trying to change it though. Between fits of violence, I would try magic. Just a week before, I had one I was pretty sure was going to work. I prepared it gradually over most of the spring, plotting the celestial chart, timing my requests with the phases of the moon. Making sure I asked each of her children on the day of the month corresponding with their birthday. It took an effort to line her five children, oldest to youngest, under the full moon in the back yard. The eldest daughter stood bored and bound by her promise after hours of pleading. Grant and Little Lyle had to be bribed, Robert threatened, and the youngest daughter was in love with me. I put my hands on their heads each in order of their birth saying nothing. Their eyes closed, the boys snickered and stood still. It was as though they'd been hypnotized. I hurried down the line, lingering on each skull as long as I dared. I cupped their faces and my fingers shook. The thought of each smooth orb passing between her legs and into my hands somehow intended to lessen the vast distance between her and me. The eldest daughter's face compressed with a hunch about this ritual. I trusted that it was beyond her imagination. She would not let the thought take shape. It was right there in front of her.

"Eddie, you are so damn weird."

The ritual ended. In the days that passed, nothing happened.

But the pressure built until I caved in Little Lyle's ribs. I bulldogged Grant's neck in my arms and flung him to the ground. I attacked Robert and knocked the air out of his chest. An older boy came to his defense and I hit him with a power I didn't ask for, didn't want, and loved more than anything in the world. I had access to something wrong and undeniable, something bad that no one seemed to have a defense against. The kid went across the street and started screaming that I was crazy. I faked a slap at Robert's ear and drove my other fist at his chest. Robert ducked; I caught him in his face. He dropped holding his mouth and his fingers turned red. He sputtered what a "thon-of-a-bith" I was. I got him to his feet and tried to get him into the canyon before he could get home to show Wanda the damage. He followed me for a few steps, then his tongue felt the hole where his teeth used to be. He freaked. I watched him walking home, each step like he was stamping out a fire in his path, his hair electric in anger.

I was ruining him. I transformed my best friend into a player in my rituals. My friendship with him was based on the beauty of his mother. I had nightmares at night and my heart pounded when I woke up. There was no excuse for me.

It was all so obvious. I couldn't understand why everyone pretended not to see it. I knew everyone needed to keep a sense of order. Mamma Bear, Daddy Bear and Baby Bear. I knew that everyone needed to play their role or they would go crazy. But I couldn't find a place for myself so I just lived. And I wanted Mamma Bear. I could feel it like an electrical charge buzzing and snapping between all of us. She must have known. I could see it in her walk, in her eyes.

There were two levels of living. One on the surface with smiles and hellos. We all went about our daily activities as if it weren't there. But there were always little giveaways to another darker hidden level. I could see it in the animosity Lyle and his wife shared.—the tightening of jaws, abrupt ends to conversations, eyes lingering on turned backs, dishes clattering with anger. I could sense it all around me.

Her sons watched us whenever we were in the same room. She stared at me for longer than she should have. She stared with curiosity. Her body spoke. I'd hold my breath as she untied the apron's knot behind her back and turned to hang it on a hook next to the door. I could feel my arms around her thin waist so clearly that she must have felt them too. Her fingers would tangle through her black hair, her forearm wiping her brow.

She whistled low looking at me and said, "Boy, it's a hot one today."

I jabbered something in response and she half-smiled, her eyes growing soft and sympathetic. Offended and angry inside, I'd leave.

I'd lay low for a few days, sleeping and trying to rest. Then I'd come back down the street and weave stories to her children. I'd tell them their secrets, infiltrate their minds and alleviate their fears with insights that I hoped would balance the violence I rained upon them. I celebrated their names, offered them views to the infinite potential hidden in us all. I won back their hearts and captured their imaginations. All the while I could feel it coming.

Then after a day or two, the emphasis would shift back to her. I'd go into her house with eyes hunting, sitting in the room pretending to nap, watching her sitting in the rocker singing softly to herself. Waiting for her tongue to part her lips. Waiting for the moment to say the funny thing that made her laugh. Waiting to say the words that meant two things. Watching her eyes look into me. Searching for the second meaning, to see if it was there. Speaking dirty things to her in my mind without saying a word.

But it always built into something that triggered me. I'd wake one morning with my eyes blazing and molars grinding. I'd get dressed and climb out my bedroom window. Making my way to her house through the canyons bordering our houses, I'd try to go along the ditch, climbing from tree to brush to tree without touching the ground. I ran over the stones on the creek bottom, went through a storm drain leading to a path behind her fence. I'd climb it and drop into her back yard. The boys would be sitting around the patio behind the garage listening to the radio. I'd have to get control of myself if a grownup was there. But if there wasn't, they'd take one look at me and run. But I was a cat and they were mice. And then I'd beat them and rampage through the neighbors' yards, breaking windows, screaming and destroying whatever was near me, defiling anything of sentimental value, spitting and fighting everybody until the they put me in my room alone to masturbate again and again.

A day or two later, I'd review the wreckage. Hearing doors close as I neared houses. Enduring anguished lectures and cowering under threats—a repentant son, a satiated angel. Inside knowing I was an animal who ruined anyone who came too close.

I could affect them all, but I could not get to her. I inspired her anger. I made her face contort with revulsion and something else that seemed like curiosity and a desire to fathom what this force was that drove me to these strange, violent lengths.

Basic conduct must have originated in the need for tribes to survive, but this was not instilled in me. I could not be overwhelmed or made to submit to any convention. I could not accept it; the face of the want was so great that I already recognized it as my own fall. I did not expect to plead to anything that had an ear toward forgiveness. Forgiveness had nothing to do with me.

There would be a price and I would pay it the moment it presented itself. But it never did. It just existed like a thing that just was, and had nothing connected to it. And over time, it faded.

Her sons paid it. They found their own needs to trust beyond instinct, to defy the truly dangerous, to risk finding something they could not understand, to go where they did not belong, to be drawn to all of those things. Before they were thirty, they were murdered in San Berdoo behind a garage by a new friend for failing to see what should have been plain to them. They had seen it before.

ALI

LI, ALI, ALI, ALI !

PULSATION WITH PRECOGNITIVE TIMING,
TRIMMED DOWN TO BARE
ESSENTIALS
NOURISHMENT TO THE SPIRIT BEYOND
SOUL
I DIDN'T KNOW WHO I WAS
DIDN'T KNOW WHAT I HAD

BEAT GETTING
FAINTER
MOMENTS LEAPING
AT ME
FROM WEEKS AGO
DENTED THUMPED

DINGED CUT
LADEN
WITH LIVING
THIS
AIN'T RIGHT
HOLLOW
INSPIRATION
PASSING BY
WITH A TELEVISION CREW

DON'T KNOW WHO I AM
DON'T KNOW WHAT I HAVE

12TH ROUND
IMAGINE THAT
I GOTTA BE
TRIPPIN'
PUT IN A PLACE THAT'S TOO HOT
AND HARD
TO BREATHE
HIT SO HARD
THEY'RE SAYIN'
I'M FROM OUTTA TOWN
THEY'RE SAYING
THE DUDE DON'T KNOW
WHERE HE'S AT

I GOTTA REACH BACK
WAY BACK DOWN HERE
A PLACE I USED TO GO
BEFORE I WENT NUMB
AND NOW WITH IT COMING BACK

I CAN GRAB SOME OF THOSE ESSENTIALS
OF LIVING
GET ON SOME OF THAT TIMING
BECAUSE
I AM
MORE THAN WHAT I DO
ALI, ALI, ALI, ALI, ALI !

WHOPPER

The truth is Robert Monroe was a liar. He was lying when I was six. He was still lying when I was ten. He needed lies in his life. He needed falsehood. He said the truth was too boring.

One morning Robert started in on a long story and this guy home from a CYA detention camp out in Poway groaned, "What a whopper," and spat through his teeth, hitting Robert on the shoulder of his t-shirt.

Robert looked at the ground in front of him for a week. Then he started telling about the time his father got his fingers slammed in the truck door, which we knew was true because we were there when it happened. That story led right into one about the day his epileptic uncle pulled a V8 out of an Oldsmobile with his bare hands. The way his eyes went red as he stood up with the whole works balanced on the inside of his forearms. How he shook, and the pressure blew his boots off.

Someone finally just started calling him Whopper. The shock on his face said he knew for sure he'd been tagged. For the rest of that Saturday, every time someone called him Whopper, everyone would crack up, rolling on a lawn under a jacaranda tree, flowers crushed under our brown backs, hysterical in the delight of such an outrageous disgrace of one of our own. Whopper kept trying to threaten us into dropping his new name but it was no use.

Didn't stop him from lying though. He'd quit for a while, then he'd get away with a little lie. Then he'd try a larger one to see if he could still pull it off. We'd bust him. He'd even cry when we didn't believe him. It got so he'd really bug you.

In July, he tried to pad his batting average and we caught him. We shouted the lie at him through the fence when he got to bat, watched him strike out. We mentioned it at the concession stand in front of his sisters. Brought it up about ten times during the long walk home after the game. He took it pretty bad. He'd want to fight, but being in the wrong, his heart wasn't really in it. We laughed at him instead.

That turned out to be his last lie. We didn't notice at the time really, but by the time we got back to school, Whopper hadn't whopped since baseball season.

First day at school at the bike racks. A cloud of dust and a deep circle of boys. Fight's gonna start. I'm walking over with Whopper beside me. About twelve sixth-grade boys are in a circle, yelling in horror. And in the center is Jimmy Johnson, the toughest sixth grader who ever lived.

Jimmy Johnson was already building a reputation that was to peak two years later in the eighth grade, when he got impatient only being the toughest kid in junior high. He wanted the high school. He made sure the word got to the toughest kid there, a Golden Gloves boxer named Matranga. Then Jimmy went right up to the guy in the middle of school and said, "Let's go somewhere where the teachers can't protect you."

That afternoon at a hamburger stand, in front of about three hundred kids, Jimmy Johnson kicked the shit out of Matranga.

Thirty seconds. It was strange to see the will of someone evaporate like it did in Matranga. Jimmy showed him a whole different level of violence. It went beyond trying to hurt someone or sensing victory or anything like that. It was without honor or logic. It was Jimmy doing what he was born to do. And when Matranga's car keys popped out of his jacket pocket, Jimmy snatched them off the ground and threw them on the burger stand roof. Jimmy yelled to his buddy Benny. Benny tossed him a can of lighter fluid. He sprayed down the guy's hair and lights him up. Whoosh! Matranga ran around like a horror movie until a couple of friends threw him down and smothered the flames. By then, Jimmy and Benny were gone.

At the bike racks, Whopper and I approach the circle and peer through the shoulders. Jimmy Johnson is down on his hands and knees, cutting the legs off of a thrashing ten inch alligator lizard. The lizard has red stubs at its tail and on one leg. Jimmy put the leg in front of the lizard's mouth hoping he'd eat it, which he didn't. Jimmy was getting ready to cut off another leg when Whopper says:

"You have to stop doing that."

Whopper is in the fourth grade, a third Jimmy's size and skinny. Jimmy Johnson's got nothing to prove. I'm standing next to Whopper, praying Jimmy hasn't heard him.

"Or what?"

As soon as Whopper begins to talk he sounds miles away.

"I'll try to kick your ass."

All the boys go "Whoooaaa" at Whopper and start laughing at him. Jimmy ignores him. Whopper says, "I mean it Jimmy."

When Jimmy presses the knife on the large joint of a hind leg, Whopper pushes past a couple of kids and shoves Jimmy over. Jimmy struggles to keep his balance, but finally falls on his back holding the lizard in the air so that it doesn't hit the ground and get crushed in his hand. He's protecting it. The lizard twists its head, snaps the air, three legs twitching and a red stump left for a tail, like the burning end of a cigar. Jimmy's getting his awkward body realigned, pressing one hand on the ground, pulling his legs under his hips, using one knee and then the other to finally stand. He seems to be waiting to hear the boys snickering behind his back. Something seems to be crying deep inside.

For the first time I notice that he's wearing big, stupid-looking hard-soled shoes, the fashion of geezers at the beach. His head is plastered with a lot of vaseline melting in the sun, his scalp visible through his very thin hair. I tried to see it all at once, but I lost it beyond a vague sympathy for the lonely awkward life of Jimmy Johnson. But he is focusing on Whopper with an expression saying, "*I'll fuck you up in a minute.*"

Then he puts the lizard back on the ground and slices off two legs. He stares at it, hunting for the connection of the lizard's fate, and his part in it as its vengeful god.

Jimmy stands up. The circle widens, like it wants to get a little distance, but at the same time it moves and shrugs and jumps and ooohs and ahhhhs and groans like it's alive. Jimmy starts punching Whopper's arms and shoulders, letting him know how hard he hits. But he doesn't try to run. So Jimmy moves in going for his head. Knots and bumps turning purple on his face, nasty gaps forming over his cheeks and eyes. And Whopper keeps swinging anyway, making Jimmy more and more pissed.

What should I do? Jump in? Get the crap kicked out of me in front of everyone? Just because Whopper feels the same thing as I do about torturing a lizard, but has the guts to do something about it? What I'm seeing being done to him, I don't want done to me.

I think fascination is not necessarily a good thing. I mean we didn't want to watch. But everyone did anyway. And we would have looked if Whopper was the lizard and Jimmy was chopping him up with an axe. It's one of those unclassified sins. You will watch. But there was something clean in it anyway, as certain uses of our spirit can sanitize anything no matter how foul, because Whopper wouldn't quit. Like he was taking it from nothing but an ass kicking and making it into something else. We waited for him to quit. We couldn't see any point not to. Except Whopper had discovered something that was beyond anything he'd ever felt. It was pure purpose. Whopper was the only one with the balls to go in. I'm not making myself clear. I mean Whopper found something—new territory, a place that he ruled, his place. I mean he was, right now, between Jimmy's knees and on the ground, but he'd get to his feet just to get pounded like no one we've ever seen get pounded.

Guys are yelling at Jimmy to quit, and Jimmy is yelling back. "Not until he does!"

Whopper keeps swinging, once or twice landing something feeble on Jimmy's face. But the little pop bouncing off Jimmy's head had so much... I don't know... *class.* Finally, Jimmy goes nuts. Blood is flying in the air, girls are crying, but Whopper only gets more determined. I mean you can see the thread of concentration. It seems kind of calm. He was definitely following something and it was changing him into someone else. Hammered at the bike racks on Jimmy's anvil like they are in it together. Like Whopper needed Jimmy to show us his heart. I can't believe what I'm seeing. My feet are buried in concrete. I just stand there. Time already stopped.

Some little kids peek in the circle and start screaming and a teacher is running over. We all scatter for different parts of the canyons. Some girls wait around to give the teacher names.

I walk home with Whopper, following him down the canyon trail, listening to him cry and catch his breath. What am I supposed to say? He must hate every one of us who didn't back him up. I would if I was him. I'd especially hate me. He always calls me his best friend. I'm even a year older. I feel two things real strong. The first is that I am proud to be walking with him. The second is that I am ashamed of myself. But at that point, the distance between us was so far that I knew he couldn't blame me. I could see that he didn't. I mean, he was pissed, but who wouldn't be? I wanted to tell Whopper everything I just told you but I can't get the words at the time and he wouldn't listen anyway. So I just say:

"Man, that was the bravest thing I ever saw."

"Stupidest."

He answers in a way that had a sort of joke behind it. One word, calling it stupid, not saying it bitter but more like I said, a joke.

I couldn't believe it. I left it alone.

He told me for awhile he hoped somebody would stop it. But when he saw no one would, he figured what the fuck.

Then he says, "Where were you?"

So I lie to him. I tell him I thought he didn't want the fight stopped. Then I go further and tell him I was thinking about helping him, but a couple of Jimmy's friends were looking at me, waiting. I knew it right away. I wished I'd never said it.

"Don't lie Eddie... Don't lie to me."

He looks like he's gonna bust me in the face. He was pretty hot and he had a lot he wanted to tell me but it's plain I wouldn't understand. Nobody would. Maybe my Uncle Adrian. But none of us Whopper's age. The rest of us will just have to wonder if we'll ever have balls.

I am as amazed at this ascension as if he had sprouted wings and lifted right up off the ground. And everything he did told me he was free now. He couldn't change it if he wanted to. I always saw him in the air from then on. I mean like, *in the air*. I noticed how he always sat in the highest place. Like on the kitchen counter, or the tree in the front yard. He began talking about parachutes and astronauts. This is gonna sound funny but he seemed kind of wise, informed or something. I mean right there, he knew more than either of our fathers or any of our older brothers. I knew it wouldn't last to tomorrow but I knew for sure that right then he could tell me about things even our mothers didn't know about men. He was in on the secret.

Whopper stands for a minute, starts to walk, mumbles and sits down. He looks at me through the bruised mush around his eyes. I check out his cuts and stuff. An eyebrow has a slit that is still bleeding. He hangs his head to see how much of a puddle he can make. He tries to write his name with the drops in the dirt. He has put a tooth through his lower lip. His cheeks are blue and black, skinned and filled with dirt. His hands are raw. He's a mess.

He stares at the skin hanging off his knuckles—bright red orange scrapes you can almost see through. He chews off a large piece in the middle of his hand.

I look back up the trail, the fence on the top of the mesa is filled with kids and teachers. They're all staring down the hill. One teacher is calling out Whopper's real name, but since we're behind a stand of manzanita, we can't be seen.

I can tell Whopper's beginning to see what he's done. It's beginning to dawn on him that it's all over. He has made it. The isolation he felt in the fight was really the isolation of his own courage.

I tell him about the fight. Some of it he didn't remember and it strikes him as funny. He laughs a couple of times. He says, "Really?" when I describe how brave and tough he was. I even tell him about how he looked changed and the anvil and all. He smiles like he thinks I'm crazy.

We walk home the long way, wondering what his mother is gonna say. I ask him if he is ever going to talk about it. It seems to me to be the only way to get something out of this for himself. He can't really just go back to being who he was. He doesn't answer.

"Because it would be so righteous if you didn't."

Whopper says, "Why?"

I don't say anything. I just hoped he'd figure it out. I can see him hiding the smile on his busted lips the color of plums. He stumbles down on the edge of a deer trail overlooking a huge patch of anise. The stuff grows all over San Diego, thickets of bamboo-like stalks with big splayed flowers—tall, sometimes eight feet. The seeds taste like licorice.

He mumbles, "Yeah, I'll act like it didn't even happen."

He practices the shrug he's gonna use when people ask him about it. Every boy and girl in school will think he is God. Still, none of us would have done what he'd done to make it that way.

It worked. At school his name became ironic, like the names they give huge guys, calling them Tiny or Half-Pint. Overnight, Whopper was a name of honor.

Except at his house, because his little brother wasn't buying it. Whopper and his little brother had problems. They hated each other and I guess I was a part of it. We did things to him we shouldn't have. He was only a year younger than Whopper but we treated him real bad. He brought it on himself because he demanded so much attention. So we used to beat him up all the time. Like one year on his birthday, we tried to set records for making him cry. We got him eleven or twelve times on his 10th birthday. And he was real hard to make cry, because he had a lot of pride and he was tough as hell. In a way, he was even tougher than Whopper. Everything we did was as far as it could go. We were masters of ridicule, and knew how to cover what hurt our feelings, and say things that would really hurt his. We didn't want it to be that way but the meanness had a life of its own. Nobody could stop it.

Then Whopper decided he needed to bridge the gulf of trust between him and his little brother. The time had come to put hate behind them and form a team of brothers, a gang. All for one and all that. It sounded like a good idea since we were getting into too much shit with the old man over all the "roughhouse crap," as he called it.

Whopper stopped fucking with his little brother, told him how sorry he was, that he was his brother and, as such, they had to trust each other. And what they needed was a ritual to restore that trust.

His brother told him, "Yeah? Well fuck you."

This went on for days. Whopper telling him that it was the most important thing in the world for him to reestablish the trust that brothers need to become men. A couple of times Whopper nearly cried. He meant it; I could see that. It was always on Whopper's mind; they just had to pass this test of trust together or they'd never become men.

Finally Whopper proposed the "ritual of trust" as he said it a million times all day long whenever he had the chance. Whopper wanted his brother to stand on the edge of the roof, with his eyes closed and his arms spread like an eagle, with Whopper standing behind him. After that they could trust each other and be true brothers... after the ritual of trust.

It took Whopper all summer to get him to listen. Around Halloween he got him to come up on the roof with him for just one minute, no blindfold, and Whopper on the far side of the roof. But his brother wouldn't go back up there, saying that was enough ritual of fucking trust for him. It took working on him day and night during Christmas vacation to get him to finally do it. His little brother was beginning to believe. I would have too. Whopper had been the perfect big brother since the fight at the bike racks.

It was the day before Christmas. There was Whopper, walking with his blindfolded brother. Whopper talking in a low quavering voice, speaking of the ecstasy of blind brotherly trust, right into the ear of his brother. He led him to the edge and told him he had to let go of his hand so that he could stand behind him. His little brother stood unafraid, free of the mistrust and hurt of the past. Ritual of trust. Solemn occasion of brothers turning into men.

They looked like angels up there, their faces in the blue sky. The winter sun glowing golden and pale behind them. I was amazed again at what Whopper had become. I knew I could rise too. I could become a man who could atone for my wrongs. I could stand up for the right things, all of that. A smile broke under the blindfold. Whopper's face went cold and he pushed his brother off the roof.

His little brother didn't believe it. He thought it was a cosmic trick. Or maybe he went into shock or was just dumbfounded, because he held his position like a diver. He did a head plant from a ten foot roof onto a cement stair. Everything slowed down. The blindfold jammed down to his little brother's shoulders, his neck disappeared, and he looked like he stood on his head for a long time before he crumpled. I swear, the noise is what made the neighbors look out of their doors. The sound wasn't like anything else I'd heard, a melon or something. I got scared, like we'd finally done it this time. Whopper was ecstatic. His arms spread like an eagle, his head cocked to one side, looking over the edge at his unconscious brother.

"Sucker."

It was plain Whopper thought he had done something important. He didn't feel the need to celebrate it with me. I don't think Whopper thought there was anyone else there. It was his thing. His brother was a part of it but it was his. I got my voice and said:

"Shit Whopper, ya killed him."

The little brother wheezed a deep breath and his eyes fluttered like mad.

"He'll be ok. Don't sweat."

As weird as it sounds, Whopper looked kind again, more like an angel than ever.

"It's the best thing I could have done for him."

I started walking and it was like the street was asleep. People were looking out of their doors. The cop across the street was frozen on his lawn with his hands on his hips and his mouth open. Nobody moved, except Whopper, who was doing a little slow spin dance with his arms spread out and his face to the sky above.

I took the long way home through the canyon bottom, winding along the edges of trickling storm ditches, slipping along mossy stones, old underwear and wads of stringy paper. I can still see Whopper on the roof, turning in that circle.

After he got out of the hospital, the little brother wore a white turban on his head until after Lincoln's Birthday. Talked like he'd been drinking for the rest of the year. Their mother never trusted Whopper again. She hardly spoke to him for a long time. Their big sister left that year for Texas. And then the years just passed like clouds and all of us lost touch.

Jimmy Johnson got killed in his second tour in Vietnam as gunner on a helicopter. Whopper got murdered in a bad drug deal. He brought his little brother along—they killed him too.

HEY KID, YER A BANGER

There's a beautiful black tile doorway leading into the Sixth Avenue Gymnasium and Boxing Club in old town San Diego. Bookmakers, sportswriters, slumming socialites, sharks, punch-drunks, pimps, trainers and fighters have been crossing its threshold since 1912. Sixty years ago, fighters coming up and going down fought just across the border in Rosarito Beach. The Hollywood elite spent summers below the border, gambling and lavishing purses heavier than anything a guy could squeeze out of the cutthroat promoters in the USA.

A bent old figure rose from the drinking fountain, wiping his lips with the back of his hand. His age suggested a crisp discolored leaf, of days when horses still rattled their carts down Sixth Avenue, when one war was won and the next three were yet to be fought.

The old man turned painfully and tottered around the outside of the ring, reeling over his collapsed hip.

Eddie looked down at his own skinny white legs swinging beneath him toward the heavy bag. He shuffled to his left, released a flurry of punches into the bag's midsection and backed up. He took a lot of pride in his speed. He figured in a few more months he'd develop a punch to go with it, and then after a little more time with the old man, maybe he'd get in the ring and see what he could do. He sensed a change in the room. His hands dropped to his sides.

A young woman stood two steps in from the front door. In the bleachers, conspiratorial heads bent closer together, eyes fixed on her. She was tiny, a perfection of hips and curves, all the more appealing in miniature because of the power that emanated from her like a contradiction. Fighters began to hit harder, dance faster. In the gallery, forced laughter rang from one corner to another. Whispers grew into audible comments. If her body understood the craving around her, she seemed oblivious to it.

Her gaze searched the corner where Eddie stood. She took a place by herself in the bleachers. Eddie turned to the heavy bag, but dropped his hands again. Embarrassed, he pretended to need an answer from the old man. He crossed the room. She ignored him, fanning herself with a folded sports section. She crossed her legs and her skirt rode to the middle of her thigh.

The old man cleared his throat.

"Yeah, kid, whatja want?"

"Oh, uh, I was wondering if..."

"...Maybe that girl in the stands is looking for a fighter?"

Eddie's face grew hot.

"No.. I uh,.."

"She's got a fighter."

"No.. I wasn't.."

Eddie lowered his voice.

"...thinking about the girl..."

"Bullshit, kid. I can see right through you. Is that what you are? Bullshit?"

"Hey, c'mon."

"I'm putting you in with Ray in twenty minutes."

Eddie's mouth opened and shut. He was not ready for Ray. He wasn't ready for anyone, especially Ray.

"That's what yer here for kid, am I right?"

Fear jumped jagged through his bones and spun in his stomach. He couldn't reply. His heart thundered.

"Isn't it? Kid?"

The old man yawned wide and turned to end the discussion, calling over his shoulder, "Twenty minutes, Kid."

Eddie made it to the heavy bag.

"Ray Starkey, you're in with Eddie Burnett in twenty minutes."

The old man's voice boomed. The bleachers responded with a flurry of activity.

Ray Starkey's voice echoed as he came out of the locker room.

"I had five rounds yesterday, Pops."

"Yer getting five more today. Twenty minutes."

"Ok, Pops. Whatever you say."

Eddie fought the urge to unwrap his hands, to take a little humiliation and leave. He tried to think up an excuse that would sound right when he'd have to explain. The room closed in.

He lost his heart. He began unwrapping his hands. He heard mumbling from the bleachers. He heard steps coming up behind him. The old man unwound the remaining twists, smoothed the wrinkled cotton and rewrapped.

"C'mon kid, just do what I taught ya."

As Eddie began to plan a way to lose like a man, the thought hit him.

"*I'm a coward. I'm too afraid to walk out of here, and too afraid to fight.*"

The old man pulled the tape tight, breaking Eddie's trance.

"I just want you to get a feel for it, see what it's like. Starkey ain't gonna kill ya kid. You'll be alright."

Eddie could hear Starkey walking down the bleachers. He heard him begin to hit the bag. The thuds shuddered through the room.

"Just use your speed to stay out of his way. I just want him to get a little tired. Just don't trade any punches with him for Christsake."

Eddie's corner faced the bleachers.

Bell.

Everything was brighter, higher, quicker. Eddie and Ray started innocently. But after the first two exchanges, they went into another world. They stepped in. They stepped up. They slugged it out.

"Hey hey, kid."

Eddie's footwork was reduced from flying strides in workouts to a shift of one inch, enough to find room to return a shot under the elbows, into the ribs, on the side of the head on the way out, all the while holding ground and absorbing the thuds and jolts of pain. The intimacy horrified Eddie.

Bell.

"Hey, kid. What the hell ya doing in there?"

Eddie waited in the corner for the second round. No stool. Headgear isn't right, gloves too clumsy to adjust it, too tight, too loose, something. When Ray connected, he might as well not have the thing on. He knew he didn't get to Ray half as much as Ray got to him. He wanted to quit. That was impossible now. He wanted to puke. That might be possible.

Bell.

Ray rushed him and pounded him backwards. Six unanswered punches landing first on his face and then falling to his neck and arms as Eddie lost ground and headed back to the ropes.

"Easy, Ray. Easy."

Eddie exploded into Ray, desperate to give him some back. A few men in the bleachers started yelling. Eddie connected, missed wild, and connected again deep into Ray's ribs.

Someone yelled, "Upstairs!"

Eddie shot a hard jab into Ray's nose and blood blew over Ray's mouth. The gym groaned. Ray went into another gear.

"Ray! Ray! Hey!"

A tide of bloodlust washed from the outside into the ring. Eddie saw the ropes beside him. His elbows drew into his body. His face dug into his gloves. A hammer was denting the bones of his forearms, banging in a slow, controlled rhythm. Ray was measuring him. Ray was setting him up. Eddie was his heavy bag.

"Kid, get outta there!"

He felt Ray move to his left. Something hurt Eddie to the point of a kind of horror. From just above his left hip, a flash exploded into the middle of his chest. His breath exploded out his mouth. His left foot left the canvas, his body rose, his mouthpiece fell. His mouth empty. He had to get out. He could not take—Another flash exploded near to the impact of the first, but his feet swept the floor and turned. Something whistled past his ear. His stomach caved in over a hot busting blast that took what little air he had. He got his shoulders square to Ray and slid along the ropes. Ray took deep breaths, waiting. He let Eddie move to the center of the ring.

Eddie realized Ray thought Eddie beneath him. Someone to punish, someone to put away and to smirk, "Nice fight," after the pats on his back were over. Eddie pulled Ray toward him, feigning collapse of nerve. Ray's pursuing shots were weak taps. He believed Eddie would retreat to the corner again. But Eddie stopped two feet from the corner and caught Ray walking into him with a right. The thumb caught him over the lips. His knuckles spun the headgear and Ray's head followed. Ray lost his balance. Eddie stood over him. A feeling similar to God standing Eddie on his feet. Ray was nearly down and Eddie knew he could hit him a lot harder if he could last long enough to see his chance. It was something joyful. A promise of what he needed from somewhere within that he never knew existed.

Eddie swung on instinct, the wrong hand. A left landed under Ray's neck. Ray regained his balance. Then Eddie threw a punch that couldn't really have happened. Ray took it on the hinge of his jaw. He dropped like a doll.

Bell.

The men in the bleachers looked at each other then shook their heads. They were still solid on Ray. Men leaned on hips digging wallets, jackets opened and money changed hands.

Voice yelling, "Ray all the way!"

"Oh! Fuck you! You want Eddie?"

"I'll give you 2 to 1! You like that kid?"

"Twenty bucks? Com'on!"

"Ray'll kill him."

A second passed. Same voice, "Anybody. 3 to 1, Ray nails him in the next two rounds!"

Eddie sick and dizzy, looked at the straw hat above the seated bystanders. The man wearing it defying them to take his bet. A small crowd of heads met over the bag of a man in the stands. The straw hat reached down and everyone started to laugh. He threw a towel in Eddie's corner. It bounced off the top rope and landed down on the floor.

Eddie nearly laughed himself. Everything stopped cold. Everything changed. Eddie knew it was a different world now. Those outside saw him but didn't want to believe it. Wanted him to fade on himself, knowing it was the only chance they had to remain above him. Eddie stared at the towel knowing that all that was behind him.

The room was loud and then it settled to silence. Ray was getting checked. Eddie wanted it over. The conversation went on. The bell should have rung. An argument. What was going on? The bell should have rung. Ray was nodding his head. Ray argued. Ray wanted more.

Bell.

Ray charged, but his heart wasn't in it. He had talked his way in. Or someone had talked him in. Eddie was part of that too. The bets were all laid against him. Everyone sat in hopeful consensus. They were calling it a lucky shot.

Eddie had a mean surprise. From the top of his shoulder down through his wrist, electricity jumped through the flesh of his cocked right arm. He tapped his left into Ray's face. Ray wanted more rib. He crouched smaller hoping to set up an uppercut. Eddie could have laughed.

Eddie shuffled twice to the left and there was Ray's huge slow head trying to turn to face him as Eddie's left hook spun his wet hair in a wild circle sending a shower down the front of Eddie's legs. Eddie planted his feet and drove a right between Ray's elbows losing half of its power. Ray nearly fell. His eyes widened and he backed up. Eddie realized the intimacy of this fighting brought with it telepathic communication. He saw Ray so clearly he could hear what he was thinking. He addressed Ray and his face responded as though he were saying the words:

Com'ere motherfucker I got this...

Another left exploded on Ray's face. Ray dropped his left glove, his eye dimmed.

...for ya.

Eddie popped up on his toes and flashed down with a right, then popped a left under his shoulder to stand him up. Then threw again with everything behind it, something crunched behind Ray's headgear and he dropped unstrung. Eddie made his way to the corner looking over his shoulder. Ray was flat on his back, one knee twitching. Eddie stared for less than half a second. In it, Eddie saw the woman in the doorway, her legs spread, his tongue soaking her.

The old man was saying something. Five words, began with, "Hey, kid..."

But the rest didn't matter. Eddie knew he could kill and it turned out to be closest to the awe of church. He wanted to get down on his knees before something and beg for an end to what evil remained in his heart. He had the knowledge of the pulpit, he wore black without being ordained. He could comfort, he could punish. He'd come close to the left hand, and he hated what it had made of him. His life had come down to one monstrous moment of self-love.

He had been there, and the guilt was branded in the beginning of any thoughts of himself. Any voice giving his life a meaning would be invalid. A declaration of love would be a tragic mistake. A long trail leading toward sudden euphoria and plunges into misery. He'd forever worship at an altar of his own making, in celebration of who he was and what that meant. The guilt was here to stay. Every time his fist closed, his hand would be empty.

BLUE

I backed into a dark room, surrounded in a hot enclosure of fog. Her eyes are feline; the soles of her shoes imbedded with little hard-earned diamonds of broken glass from broken streets, reminders that you can leave but something comes with you.

Her mouth is on mine. She brings tears to my eyes when she bites here for a second, letting up to give a second's relief, the pain reverberating and then gone. Like a message about the events of what is before us, what lingers, what passes. She's always immediate, like storms, prides, packs, tribes. She is insistent, demanding. Why does this make me think of forgiveness, of solitude, of a state of grace?

Androids watch us from another room. Shafts of light give their features razor angles, lending any expression an amplification. A smile is the baring of teeth. Repose is a judgmental stare, a long look a century to come. Past caring. Travelers beyond our time. They turn in unison. One throws open a window and begins to sing a dirge over the cracked and bleeding streets.

She wants to get me off, to put me someplace safe, someplace I have been in collected seconds over my past decades—a place I belong. She pushes me further into the room, into the deeper shadow. Her laced boot, with a galaxy glinting in her soul, kicks the door closed. Her hand gripped tight and me thinking.

"*I've never let anyone jerk me off.*"

Never had a hand on me, and her grip remains the gravest and most hopeful coming death and sacred send off. I look at my hand stretched out before me catching the light. I see through the skin. Cables pull at muscle. Blood rushes in, presses out, rushes in. I put my hand over my eyes.

I'll never come. Her mouth breathes hot, and in her chest, a groan rises like lava up the vent of a volcano, bringing the message and another burning bite. I wonder if this is coming... if this is coming... if this is coming, while her hips rock and her grip tightens. My cheek is between her teeth and her warm spit splatters on my face timed with groans that can only mean, to my amazement, that getting me off will get this sweet girl off.

And I can't think anymore, something takes over. Is this coming... is this coming... is this coming, and I give it up. I go blind. I leave all things behind, and Baby Girl who can cut you in, or cut you out, opens her soft eyes and I'm not making sense saying:

"Red tide. Sticky when you get out. Most people don't like it. Glows in the dark."

And she asks, "Glows in the dark? Really? Never heard of it."

The Androids lean against the door, their weight creaking the floorboards.

And I say, "Yeah, glows in the dark. Really beautiful."

I'm glistening under a street lamp, shining like a smeared star. Blue like the lonely moon.

WEAK

I was in withdrawals. The sound of sixty thousand people celebrating a catch that you weren't sure you could pull off is a rush that is hard to duplicate. Waiting under the lights for a kickoff to drop out of the sky in the clear cold night, the adrenaline coursing through your legs as you run on instinct, making a cut here and dodging a flying assassin there, is an experience that every young man ought to have. The beauty of it is that so few do.

Walking into the stadium before a game, high on a handful of bennies, headphones raging "Exile on Main Street". Anticipating a night where anything is possible. Abject failure and injury or the pinnacle of accomplishment. The come-from-behind victory. Circus catches and the party afterwards. The women getting you a beer; the guys hanging around laughing and coming down with a few joints. Driving out to the beach with Diane, feeling the aches begin as the adrenaline wears off. Listening to the radio, hearing the news broadcast announcing the touchdowns you scored and the smile you just couldn't hide. An ego thing that you have no choice but to give in to because it is just too cool. And you want more. You want it to go on forever. Keeping it going at the big relay meets in the spring. Running down someone with a lead like they are standing still and the crowd on the fence screaming their heads off.

You can't stop. It's a life so full of camaraderie, challenge and adrenal/ego rushes that it's hopeless to consider quitting. You just keep going until they say you can't play anymore or you just aren't fast enough.

The echoes of roaring stadiums still haunted me. But it was gone. I fed the memory like an addict. I couldn't let it go. But I wasn't playing anymore, and the next step up was the pros or the Olympics. I was a husband and a father, splitting time between trying to be a man and wanting to be a boy again. I was living in the past, certain that I could still pull it off if I had taken the chance, if I'd believed in myself just a little more. Getting high enough to fantasize victory at one more Olympic trials, or walking into pro camp and fighting my way in. Getting it worked out in my mind, rolling another joint.

I was living in Los Angeles. Rubbing elbows with hipsters fresh from the Rolling Thunder Revue. Hanging out with movie stars, hard-time fallers, ascenders, heroes, saints, whores, gypsies. All of them dying piece by piece. All of them tough enough to laugh it off.

I was just hanging out, carrying what I thought was my own weight. Included in the tribe of dervish angels. Invited to the party, in on the shit in the back room. Watching the big dice roll and the bloody knuckle closing the nostril over some of the most beautiful smiles in the world. Around sundown on a porch overlooking the private beaches of Malibu, celebrating a friend's Academy Award. Watching the pelicans coasting and sliding the troughs of breakers, the sun dropping like Icarus into the blue horizon. Cocktails clinking, faces all over the place competing for the funniest line, the coolest vibe, looking for the best sex. Everybody hallucinating on fame, wealth, power and every drug you can name. The sweet, sticky taste of marijuana still on my teeth, another joint between my fingers.

Getting all the mileage I could from my athletic past. Not knowing that it is part of the mystery and bullshit of Angelenos to make each other larger than life. I believed it, never guessing that no one paid any attention to what anyone said. It was just a huge mutual adoration society. The echoes of the past making it all seem so much like the reality of the stadium. I'd done the impossible with my body; there was no need to suspect that I hadn't earned the acceptance and backslapping exclusivity of Hollywood too. Besides, I knew I had a right to anything Movieland had to offer, that the doorman at the gates to Olympus would recognize me and usher me right through.

There was a big league pitcher hanging out with the hipster underground. Everybody knew his name. Everybody talked about his eccentric tendency to drop a couple hits of acid, go out to the mound and retire the side for a few innings until a laughing fit brought the manager out to point the direction to the dugout. On this afternoon, he was standing next to me listening intently. He wanted to know my story. Wanted to know what had become of me, what had happened, why I had dropped out of sight.

I explained. I told him about the war and how I couldn't stand to compete in front of those masses of Americans wanting me to run down their racist white hope dreams for them. How they wanted me in the big stadium, the biggest game. The Games. Representing apple pie, Mom, and the goose step. How I couldn't keep time with the mindless lemmings jack-booting through suburbia. I pretended an acceptable level of modesty, smiled when he suggested I'd have undoubtedly made it to Montreal. After that, the pros would be almost automatic. I mentioned that the scouts for Dallas, Oakland, and Green Bay had all shown interest. He mentioned the names of my old teammates who were working in the pros now. How I could have done it. Yeah, it was in the bag. I sighed with a kind of weighted resignation. But the war, and the stands full of Nixon backers, and the higher moral ground was so elevated that the events on the field just didn't really justify coming back down. I was just so... illuminated up there beyond the clouds that shade those mortals beneath us who just couldn't understand the pressures and the hopes pinned on us by the fans. I had a responsibility to reject and to live beyond the definitions of competition. I was in it for the art and not for the winning or losing. That competition is a metaphor for warfare, and with Vietnam raging, I felt used. I wanted to create great races. I was into transcendence, not out to see who was the better man.

I rolled another joint. I had more to say. The pitcher smoked it with me and I went on. He asked me more questions and I went deeper into my logic. I found new levels of brilliant insight into why I was better than the production of my abilities, beyond the crass expression of my god-given talent. I finished.

He looked at me and said, "That's so weak." And he walked away.

SLIDE

I'm so spaced in the early morning sun that the question is not where am I, but where will I puke next.

Right here.

My stomach contracts in a single spasm. It's mostly spit. I see a lawn sprinkler and follow the green snake to the spigot, turn it on and return to the splashing puddle in the dirt. The cold water uses my stomach as a trampoline and flies up and out of my mouth. I breathe a little air, then what's left in my stomach blasts out of my nose. Alright, I'll wait.

I circle around like a dog and pass out, curled on my side in the hot sun. I hear voices, tiny and deep from within a cave somewhere in Africa. But when I open my eyes, there are tips of roughout boots in front of my nose. The voices are discussing what to do about me. They're what pass as friends. Big guys who try, and succeed, at making people shit themselves. Last image I can think of is a shotgun in some fuckup's mouth as he gets the time and date straight for his last chance.

We're supposed to be planning the details of setting up a black funk soulster superstar who has a tendency to go off behind cocaine.

The object, of course, is to get the funkster's coke and money without getting caught, which would mean getting killed. I had a plan to use two sure things: greed and ego. Get him to overextend himself and then get him irrational when he tries to cover his embarrassment. But before I could work out the cast of characters, I got drunk.

So far, the plan calls for me to deliver a pound and hang around in the front room, waiting for someone to get back from somewhere with a lot of money, and then stall until my friends come in and take us all off. The pretext is women and some problem with airline tickets.

Then my job is not to freak out while all these psychos strut around and try to fuck with me. It's a delicate balance between knowing how much to take and where to draw the line. My bit is stupidity. I am the butt of jokes, conversations going on around me that I shouldn't be hearing, gleaning this, figuring that, then doing something off the wall. It's worked in Mexicali, Juarez, El Centro, San Ysidro, El Cajon and Santee. Now we're gonna give it a try in Malibu.

I'm getting to my feet, listening to my friends argue about my condition. Standing up blinds me for a second. The top of my head comes to their chests. They must weigh two hundred and fifty pounds apiece.

"I'm ready."

I expect the laughs. Here they are. Laughing, then silence. One guy is about to utter a challenge. I can tell because he's from the South, and he telegraphs his hostility by curling his lip—Elvis damage. I interrupt him.

"I'm more effective when I'm underestimated."

He's about to say something devastating to my interests. I edit the movie playing in my head which stars him in an amazing scene of beating me to a humiliated pulp. The estimates of his weight are ignored behind the central thing in my mind, which is hit him real hard and real fast. Then as he recoils, swarm him. When those thoughts get strong enough, the imagined action follows. Guys are pulling me off and I am praying my target is unconscious. Hit him twice and no one saw the punches. Believe me, if you have the choice between size and speed, take speed. He's doing a little half turn. His upper body is out before his knees know it. He's buckling backward with his knees still trying to hold him up. Finally his heels flick out in the dirt and his back thuds.

I start to walk toward the car saying, "Let's stop for breakfast." We cram ourselves into a Valiant and drive off.

Beautiful Malibu flying past the open windows, a joint fired and passed around. Going up to Trancas to rip off a superstar. This is the life. Except the radio... that seventies music—weird, imitative, overproduced stuff. Right now, the Eagles are flying or something, and then someone is running down the road trying to loosen something with women on his mind.

Driving through empty Malibu, up carless Pacific Coast Highway on a hot spring Wednesday makes you feel like you're getting away with something. There's the ease of residential opulence; the only faces you see are locals, and most of the locals are stars, near-stars, were-stars, know-stars, want-to-be stars, think-they-are stars, sexual-partners-to stars, suppliers-of-vice-to stars, parasitic-servants-to stars. And on the road blasting past, you almost think you're rich and famous. Actually you think you're too cool to be famous. Especially if you have Phoenix Program washouts riding with you who manage to kill a couple people a year.

Killers suck the air out of the room, but you have to look close to notice. Intense implies some kind of action or energy. What these guys have is a complete absence of energy which they try to cover up with an act. Like the funny wheezy guy in Pacific Beach, the sharp dressing Romeo hair-combing guy from San Ysidro, the four-eyed school teacher who always reads the dictionary to improve his vocabulary, and dumbshit losers carrying piano wire, plumber's wrenches and hammers like the ones I'm riding with. Their guns are inside the spare tire in the trunk.

The guy driving changes channels looking for Willie on the country station. These guys will damn near cry if they hear Willie singing "Somewhere Over The Rainbow". That's almost as scary as the weird scratching habits and teeth sucking sounds they're always making.

The highway is dead. Everything is going on behind the walls that line a five mile stretch of PCH. You can grab a glimpse of beach between a restaurant and a gas station. Other than that, it's a rolling line of walls to the west. Behind each one, somebody famous getting sucked by somebody who wants to be. Ok, that's jaded, cynical. Every other wall.

Eventually the Spanish tile is left behind. Pass the hidden gates of the Colony, home to huge money and temporary power. The whole place is paranoid. Neighbors never speak except in hails called across the street. Everybody busy with the effects of the latest hit, or big deal, or heavy meeting, or this or that. Usually just pantomimed cool.

"Yeah, bitchin. Thank you, thank you. We are all stars together here. Isn't it just wonderful in the cool terrace and tile hallways in this I'm-scared-to-death-to-get-older-smaller-less-powerful-land? Yes, yes, no autographs here. We are all stars."

All said in waving hands, cool shade tilts, and casual hundred thousand dollar car-door openings. The scared-to-death part reserved for shrinks, or as confessionals to appear human enough to get somebody's pants down. Out here on the narrow Colony streets, it's strictly the celebrity benediction, neither one believing the other. Some remnant of the papal wrist swinging acknowledgment of access to the high and fucking mighty.

Breakfast is on me. The waitress is in worse shape than we are. She's cranky and nauseated with a healing rope burn on her wrist, nose ring, blond hair, cigarette dangling, eyes patrician and smug, body dreamed up by a fuckbook artist before the age of surgery. See-through cotton dress. Her girlfriend arrives, sits on the inside of her ankle, leans over the counter. Twists the counter stool, left beaver shot, right, left beaver shot, right. Blinding me like a lighthouse beam. Hard to concentrate. Anticipation for the next twist, attempting to keep from being busted. As if she doesn't know. As if she fucking cares.

I'll take half a dozen scrambled eggs. Steroids need that extra protein. I rattle three little blue pills out of a plastic brown bottle—Dianabol—discovered by farm boys who wanted to make the team out in Texas and found out the meat their daddies put on a steer could be the meat they put on themselves for the Cotton Bowl. People will tell you steroids create a feeling of invincibility. I'll tell you, a couple months on a steroid cycle, and if a cop car gets too close, you'll rip its door off. Makes you horny, too.

Up on my feet heading for the lighthouse. Big smile. No response. Under-my-breath request for a couple of lines. Girl never looks at me. I take the little envelope that materializes out of her hip pocket. My Frye boots galump toward the bathroom. Her voice sounds like Jodie Foster accepting the Deepest Voice in America Award.

"Sixty bucks."

I'm still thudding my heels toward the men's room, slow and steady like a gunfighter. Sometimes I act like that if a woman blows me off and makes me disgusted at myself, I should just tell her I want attention.

"Hey, I said sixty bucks."

She's used to being paid attention to. This is a contest of wills. I'm in the men's room. She's in the men's room. I lock the stall door behind me. She's coming over the top of the stall. She's pissed, yelling this amazing shit at me. I say, "Go ahead," to all her threats throwing in, "I hope you do," to a couple of her suggestions. Envelope is open; she's pulling my hair above the toilet tank. One of my friends is laughing a beery, bluster-boy haw haw. She's getting tired and isn't yelling. She's hissing, "son-of-a-bitch-mother-fucker" at me. Fingernails in my scalp. Alright already.

"Hey hey hey... Here, take it. I was just kidding."

She pushes me around the stall.

"Asshole."

Yeah, sorry, I know. She fills a spoon, puts it under my nose. Boom. Malibu dentist's daughter I guess.

By the time we get to Trancas, the funkman has departed. He's living elsewhere. His parties have come to the attention of the police. His guest's drunk driving has become a problem for tourists. The general scene is turning sour. I'm getting this from a guy who feels important for a second, having all this information about a famous hipster-superstar. I gotta put up with it. It's pretty warm today; all the windows are open and this guy is wearing one of those huge knit hats that flop down around one shoulder. He's wearing tight, tight, tight pants. It's plain to see it hurts him to move, but he must think it's worth it. His shirt has huge wet rings under each arm. Little drops are running rivulets down his shiny black neck. He walks back and forth across the deep shag rug, sniffing deep with a knuckle pressing first one then another nostril closed.

"Where is he? We're late already with this and my man said he was pissed."

He ignores me.

"Ok, well, when he asks about it I'll just... What's your name?"

He sneers at me.

"Ok, I don't need to know your name. I'll just say you said that he should fuck himself."

He starts telling me about my white ass.

"Let's just drop the racial shit, ok?"

He's not listening.

"Ok, ok... right before you get to the part about the last four hundred years and all, why don't you just call Adolph?"

He asks me who the fuck is Adolph.

"Adolph is the man who takes care of your boss."

He yawns and tells me the studio is in Oxnard. He bought a house. It's better for him out there—no white folks hanging around. God, the guy doesn't quit. I ask him if it's near Pt. Mugu. He says it is. I ask if it's around the Angels' place and he says it's across the fucking street. I tell him thanks and if he talks to his meal ticket, which he will, to tell him we're on our way.

"What do you mean, meal ticket?"

"Just tell him."

Oxnard is where the pigs, like all pigs, will look the other way after their taste. We get up there past Pt. Dume, around the corner of a huge rock along the highway, and we meet a few friends at a little bar for a couple of beers. We try to see if our program is together, but it's hopeless. We can't remember anything, so we decide to play it by ear. A couple of guys stay at the bar and we call the Angels. We ask one of them to go across the street to see if anyone's home. He comes back saying there is. That, it turns out, was probably our mistake. Angels are so fast. I mean, you give them a half second to fuck something up for you and next thing you know you're saying, "Ow, Ow, Ow."

We drive over and watch three big dogs' heads pogoing over a redwood fence. After a minute or two of standing around timing our spit and the dogs' heads, we hear a whistle and the dogs are rounded up. A man asks us what we want and we try to sound like gangsters in an old movie but we start laughing. The fence gate opens. An old black man looks at us. He's got to be the funkman's father. He lets us in, closes the gate. He's a little drunk... and he's holding a gun.

"You funny guys?"

"You drunk?"

"Yeah, you funny?"

"Where's your son?"

"Which son? I got eight."

"Oh, c'mon..."

"You crazy?"

"Yeah, sometimes."

"Sometimes" hits the old man's funny bone. He doubles over. I get embarrassed. I feel my face getting red. I knew right there that something was real wrong.

The patchy lawn is dotted with white and brown piles—every square inch. The place stinks. The door to the house is wide open. Doris Day is singing "Que Sera Sera" over a zillion dollar sound system. An Amazon crosses the doorway. Three inch platforms puts her about eight feet tall. After she leaves, it takes an extra ludicrous second for her butt to clear the doorway. A voice comes from inside, whiny, and at the same time, trying to be demanding. It's a man's voice squeaking like a neurotic queen. It's the kind of voice that has no power but instead wears you down—a "with-it" smart ass assuming a superior position over somebody.

My eyes adjust to the darker room. A little white guy is sitting on the sofa. Blousy shirt, sunglasses. Guy talks fast—East Coast—makes a point of using it. Trying to conjure up mean ass streets to someone over the telephone. I hate that shit. I begin to realize he's doing a version of what he thinks is Mick Jagger. A lot of these guys are doing that androgynous bad boy bit these days. He knows he has my attention and carelessly lets a little English lower class nasal snarl rise at the end of his sentences. Fake people busting themselves everywhere.

He's a mogul of some kind, using the funkman's name. It begins to dawn on me that he is directing this stream of abuse to the funkman. He's screaming now about money, then a couple insults. Whoa, personal insults. Definitely impressive.

I walk out the door because I'm too stupid to be impressed. He'll have to try something else. The Amazon clomps up behind me. Eight feet easy. She's talking to the guys and wearing a loose halter top. When's she gonna bend over? Five... six... seven. Bend. Big jolt when the cleavage shakes loose for a good glimpse. Up... big smile. Phoenix Program licks his lips. The other guy drags a few thinning strands of what was once a pompadour through his fingers and does something like a smile or smirk with his mouth. I stuff my hands in my pockets and turn to see if the guy is off the phone. His hands are waving in the air, bouncing up and down on the sofa with each accented threat. There's no telling which continent he grew up on now. He's a cheesy Londoner one phrase and a cheesy Brooklynite the next. He gets quiet and listens. I better fall for his big shot routine.

The Amazon is telling Elvis damage where the funkman is. Blue mountains outside of Kingston or recording at Muscle Shoals. Someplace, you know how it is, never can tell. He is making a point of looking directly into her halter top. She emphasizes that funkman is elsewhere one too many times. Elvis is going to lose his balance rocking forward on his toes.

I'm back inside. The international big-shot is off the phone and now he's assuming I'll be interested in his problems with superstars. How it's so hard to make them do things when they already have more of everything than they know what to do with. Basic business, a deal is a deal and you gotta be where you say you're gonna be. Yeah... right, I understand.

I cut him off before he starts the standard rhapsody beginning with, "Well, he's a genius," and blah blah blah.

I stand still and ask can I use the phone.

"Sure, go ahead."

He glowers down at the coffee table. A gigantic ashtray is heaped with butts. He lights up. I leave a number out of my home phone. I start talking.

"He's not here." Wait...

"He's in Kingston... I guess so."

I ask the mogul his name.

"A guy here named Phil has just been talking to him."

"I don't know."

I check to see if Phil is biting. I direct a question to him.

"Phil, do you know when he's coming back?"

Phil shrugs with disgust.

"No telling... What should I do? Bring it back or what?"

Phil sits up on the edge of the couch. I turn to pretend to try and get a little privacy. He stands up and walks to the fireplace and gets a little box from the mantel. He's nonchalant as all hell about it. The phone is gonna make an off-the-hook tone any second.

"Well... shit, I don't really know. You want to talk to Phil?"

Phil turns walking with his hand out for the phone.

"Ok... then listen. I'll just see what he wants me to do. The money? Yeah, I know."

I hang up. Phil looks a little miffed.

"Phil, Adolph says you can take the load if you want to pay for it all now or get a taste on account to get you through until he gets back from Kingston. What you want to do?"

Phil's dreams are coming true. He says, "I'll take it all now."

He can barely contain himself. I say ok and Phil goes upstairs, saying anxiously, "I'll be right down."

This is a bad situation. Phil doesn't know me. He's ready to pay out a ton of money? Sure. He's ready to set us up before we set him up is what he's ready to do. The Amazon selling funkman's whereabouts tells me he's probably upstairs. This house isn't permanent; he'd never live near the Angels. He's got something going with them, some kind of split. Pretty soon the place is gonna fill up with people. They'll try to fuck up my team.

I walk out to the porch. I look at the guys.

"Let's go."

Just a little direct to Elvis, just a little "gotta go now" in my voice. Over his head. He's watching a carload of women unloading by the gate.

The Amazon is playing with the attack dogs in their cage. "Big boy. Tough boy. So vicious." The guys take it as a hinted invitation. Upstairs, a couple of Angels we know stick their heads out of windows and howl cheerful greetings to us. How the fuck we been? Jokes about watermelons to the black women walking toward the house.

If I press the guys to leave, I'm fucked. I start yelling to the guys upstairs about who's buying the beer. Not them. I collect about ten dollars from people at the front door. I swing my leg over a Schwinn and thunk thunk thunk off the porch steps on a beer run. I leave the guys there.

Out the gate, heading west to find a car to steal or a ride to hitch, whichever comes first. My friends are going to be dosed with big, cringing, paranoiac versions of every nightmare they ever dreamed. What the payback is about must have happened before I got here or maybe this is something initiated by them. The end result is the same. They'll get buried alive in the desert and no one will ever hear from them again. Tied up and thrown in a deep hole, covered over. They'll scream their heads off. They won't gag them. They'll let them talk, let them cry, let them beg, let them scream. I hear he does the digging himself. Has to do with who the baddest man in the valley is, and I guess in this case, it's the guy with the shovel. He's gonna get a ton of blow, kill two guys, and has the other one pedaling like a bastard for home. A good solider would sneak the coke out of the trunk of the car. Too close a call and I don't have the keys.

There's a party up Decker Canyon. I know this guy. I can't call him a friend, nobody can. He's just finished a movie and is hanging out spending his millions on what you can guess.

He's the most photogenic young god in Hollywood. Redford won't work with him. He carries the bad boy mystique to a point approaching realism, beyond what anyone in Hollywood has done in years. And that's saying something with all the freaks, degenerates, and homicidal maniacs that have been burning their images in the world's brains for the last fifty years or so.

Bruce Lee has been up there for about a week, hanging around and impressing the girls. Conceited little fucker. Don't tell him I said so. Anyway, you've heard about the parties and what all goes on there. He throws the lowest, most barbaric of parties, in lavish style, making it glamorous. And to go with that, he's got a lot of big wave riders around. *Big waves*, not to be found in California. The kind in Hawaii, over coral that no one in their right mind challenges. Except them. And they know it. Four or five of them up at the star's house. Idols and legends all high and happy. Pulling dozens of the most amazing eighteen year-olds you've ever seen. Sprinkled with these fearless women and musicians, or songwriters and actresses, or camera operators who are in their thirties and irresistible if they decide to focus a second or two on you. Everybody fucking 'til the cows come home.

Everything bigger than life and so comfortable with the servants cleaning the slop in seconds. The pool drained of puke, filled and reheated by Mexicans in uniform. Great parties, even if those fucking guys from the Eagles are always hanging around.

But the immediate problem is getting out of Oxnard. Nobody is gonna go too far out of their way, but if they happen to run across me, or if they pin me on their way to funkman's place, or if... Jesus, this is the real concern, if they see me on their way to the desert... Well fuck it... That isn't likely to happen for at least a couple of hours. Meanwhile, I'm thinking all this to avoid thinking about pedaling the Schwinn to the parking lot, which is a lot further than I thought and I'm getting real hot and tired. And I need the motivation before I say, "Fuck it" and stop off someplace and get nailed on account of being this lazy fuck, which is what I am. I can't tell you how many guys are sitting around in the slam because they took too much time doing this and that, or stopping off to get a little, or you know, just procrastinating instead of doing the right thing. The right thing is to get out of here.

Too late. Camaro grumbling toward me... or is it... No... probably not... Yep. It is.

The Camaro pulls to a stop, blocking my path. Nothing but fields around. I can outrun them if I have to.

"Fuck face." He's talking to me.

Doors on either side of the car swing open; three guys pile out. What is all this hostility about? They got on bathing suits, big baggy things about down to the knees, flower prints, big bellies on two and the other—Mr. Washboard. They must be ready to do something; they got the strut going. Why do guys strut? Jesus, like they got a hard-on down the pant leg, or just a dick so huge it has to be dragged behind them or I don't know what.

I'm sitting astride the Schwinn trying to look as confused as I can for the benefit of the tough guy walking real fast, one foot hitching and then sliding and then hitching and sliding. And because they're moving fast, they gotta hop along sideways in order to keep the strut. Looks so stupid. But they're serious, I can tell. One of them is looking over his shoulder for traffic. Highway Patrol always uses this cut off.

I lay the Schwinn down on its side. A butterfly darts in and out of the spokes. Every time something violent happens or is gonna happen, I see a butterfly flitting around. I remember being in a football game once and right down the line of scrimmage goes this little white butterfly. Made the whole scene seem stupid. Another time, I got jumped by about a million black dudes. They got out of their car, left the doors open, and with the radio blaring "My Girl", they tap danced on me and my friend's heads. A moment filled with irony, because at the time, that was my favorite song. That bass line and vocal became the soundtrack to our ass kicking. I thought it was so weird at the time. No butterflies, but a butterfly type of irony. Anyway, here they are. Back to you in a minute.

"Nice. Calling me fuck face."

His fist passes over my head. His balance is overcommitted and he's over the Schwinn. Good, shove him onto it. He gets tangled in the chain and sprocket, tries to keep his clumsy balance but fails. He's down.

"Hey, what is all this about?"

Better not wait for an answer. One guy has long hair. Why do tough guys wear their hair long? I'm swinging him around by it and the other guy can't get in. My knee hits his face, not too solid, just enough to double up his adrenaline. He's grabbing for a hand hold on the top of my pants. He's got me. Thumb hard in his eye. He lets go and grabs his face. I plant two shots on the back of his ear. Bingo. His body stiffens and he drops on his face. The third guy trying to get me down has just torn a long trail of skin off my back with his fingernails.

Fat fuck has just gotten to his feet. He's bouncing up and down with his fists prepared like a goddamn pugilist, all darty in-and-out and all showy. Pussy. I'll get him later. Mr. Washboard has a piece of wood from some farmer's fence. I see a guy coming from the Camaro with a tire iron. I am out of here.

Mr. Washboard breaks the wood over my head. Dry rot, nothing to it. But it's the thought that counts, right?

There are times when the universe works against you. When guys much like yourself are doing a job on you and you know that the sun and moon have had some kind of convergence and the planets are set up for a spinning red light and the wail of your ambulance.

But you never can tell, so you lead with a right that has your body behind it from the tips of your toes through your hips that were low to begin with and everything is lined up perfectly so that you're gonna break your fist or break a face. And then the guy contributes to the beauty of the moment. They call it "walking into a punch."

Mr. Washboard actually runs into this one. I never felt a thing, like connecting perfectly on a baseball and knowing immediately that it's out of the fucking park. So you can drop the bat and do that long look of admiration that the other team hates and watch the ball disappear. To top it off, I had a perfect view. I felt my fist caving into his nose, heard the sound like a chicken leg breaking. Down he went.

What you gotta do when you're gonna get hit like that is give them the top of your head. It'll hurt you but it will also disintegrate the guy's fist and probably break his wrist too. Mr. Washboard must have been doing sit-ups when he should have learned about taking a punch.

Still have to consider the tire iron. Fat fuck is not jumping around anymore; he's admiring my shot on Mr. Washboard, who is twitching on the ground with what looks like serious central nervous system damage. I feel so fulfilled. Time has just kind of stopped here for awhile.

I know there is an ethic against running away from a fight. And although I'm hot and bloodied from the battle and all, and I want to stay because of something stupid I have learned, I am also calculating. I deduce that the tire iron, plus the fat boxer, and maybe another guy getting off the ground are more than enough to kill my ass.

I'm already booking fifty yards across the bright yellow field. Mustard plants are snapping at my legs as I drive past, pollen from their heads exploding on me. Just jetting toward another road a half mile away, hoping to avoid a ditch here or a trench there. These guys will never catch me on foot. I hear the Camaro screeching off somewhere. I hope they don't have a way to head me off.

Just then the terrible things I do to my body begin to catch up with me. I'm gonna faint. No doubt about it. I stagger down to my hands and knees and try like hell to stay conscious. Nope, I'm gonna take a little nappy right here. The last thing I remember is rolling over on my side in a giant field of tall mustard plants. Everything settling down dark and quiet, the hum of a thousand of bees all around me.

I heard later that the Camaro guys drove around for about an hour and the last place they thought I'd be was sleeping in the field. Maybe there is a God. Think so?

Anyway, around Christmas the next year, one of the guys in the car bought me a few pitchers of beer and told me the tale. Fat fuck boxer guy was married to a woman I had been in bed with a week or so earlier. What he didn't know and should have, was that she brought me home with one of her girlfriends. I was finished in about a half hour or so, but the girls went on all night. I couldn't get any sleep at all until I moved to the couch and I still couldn't sleep with all the racket. I think I made their scene hetero or something. When she had to confess her infidelity, she left out the part about the girlfriend. To the fat guy with his hurt feelings, I looked like some rival.

In the late afternoon, the temperature in the field changed abruptly. The wind shifted bringing in the fog, which revived me. Headache. Worse than that... Intestinal volcano.

I hitched down to the coffee shop. Invited the waitress to the party. She gave me a ride. Slept it off. The night pretty uneventful.

Next day at about three in the afternoon we're having breakfast, sitting in some kind of breakfast nook, sunlight filtering in through the windows. Antique carved table with every kind of fruit, roll, exotic breakfast thing you can think of. There's the movie star I told you about, the big time surfer I told you about, and the movie star's wife. She is trying hard to hold her family together.

They have a five month-old daughter. Mine is about a month and a half younger. His wife is pretty cool, but in what you might call denial. She thinks things are in some way alright; she thinks they have a family. It's pretty sad. The sadness carries over to me. I have a wife. I have a baby girl and I'm out doing all this shit all the time. Stuff they'll never know about, because once I get it together, I'll rescue them and we'll live the good life and I'll have this colorful past to season myself with. I'll be like a retired pirate, or like Turner in that Nicholas Roeg movie, so that I won't be some kind of weakling that kissed ass and got to be this big success at whatever it was I was fantasizing about at the time.

But right there at breakfast, things changed. I was still thinking I'd be a star somehow, since I was sitting there with one, and he wasn't any real big deal, and he liked me and probably would use me in his next action movie because I was the real deal and blah blah blah... So I rolled a few joints and listened to the stories about the movie these guys had just finished. Location in Mexico. About surfing and the dynamics of all the personalities, and the challenge, and the American values of men against nature and against the nature of themselves, and overcoming themselves to find a higher meaning for life as the sun sets on the giant waves that they surf to change their lives and learn about the beauty of the world and the stuff that Hollywood wants you to believe.

Meanwhile, behind the scenes they're doing all the drugs a pickup truck can deliver to the set and fucking anything that moves. These guys do get girls—women, wives, duchesses, singers, writers, brilliant talents and hard living, hard loving babes. This is their reality; this is how they live. The wives look the other way, not to forgive, but to blind themselves to it. Like I said, denial. Which was where I was at, since I was never gonna be any goddamn star. I was a sort of joke to myself, but I didn't want to think that anyone else could see it. You should learn it now; if you can see it in yourself, then so can everybody else. There are no secrets, only delusions.

So they started comparing the girls to dogs. The ones they had, you know, they'd think up a poodle here and Doberman there. All bringing laughs. The surfer guy commented about the Chihuahua that my movie star friend had, cause she was so little.

He looked at me, winking the sensimilla out of his eye and tapping the ash, passed me the joint. His face was real handsome for that moment, and it had a bitchin' looking killer sneer on it. It was easy to see why he was a movie star. He did a cool quick take over his shoulder to see if his wife could hear. The baby was patting the table in his lap and he looked at me real deep and knowing and said:

"More like a Mexican hairless."

Hmmm. I felt my shoulders shrug, not getting it at the moment. But then I got it. He liked them young.

I felt like making everything right again. Going back to a place that wasn't full of shit, cleaning it all up. But I knew I couldn't without destroying myself along the way. I'd have to stay this way a little longer, being in the habit of it, having what you'd call my identity a part of it.

I got up from the table and walked back home.

I lay on top of my roof, under a huge sycamore tree, with my baby girl sleeping on my chest. Wondering if I could get back what was left of my soul.

THE DESOLATE AMBITION
OF FOREGONE FAILURE

eartless strokes pumping my saltless blood
back to the same cold chamber.

My limping strides following a giant's rain-filled prints,
as the breath is hard to find and my spirit is dying.

God damn this.

REACH

Eddie was walking until he found train tracks. He was drunk and feeling disillusioned. His youth was long gone, nothing could replace it. He'd pretty much screwed up his relationship with his daughter and wife. He turned out to be one of those men who secretly resented the ones he loved. They were in the way of his self-destruction, of living a way that had a few thrills to it. He hadn't turned out to be one of those men who uses the ones he loved as a means for self-ruin. He loved them more than that. It was himself he was beginning to hate.

Eddie had a hypothesis that he was trying to prove. He'd waited until the women were gathered in the kitchen, since he didn't drink anymore, to spin the top off his Tequila bottle. He hit it, and passed it to the guy next to him saying, "If they ask, tell 'em I'll be right back."

The guy rehearsed. "Said he'd be right back."

Walking down the driveway, he sang under his breath.

"*I've grown so used to you somehow. Well I'm nobody's Sugar Daddy now...*"

His wife was cheating on him. He was cheating on her. His

daughter knew it. He was determined to make it out to the tracks. In ten minutes, his boots crunched over the gravel in the train yard. Along the way he'd reached back to some of the music of long gone days, when he sat next to his uncle in his old three-quarter ton International pickup. Those were cowboy songs mostly, but his Uncle Adrian would stomp along with one of Sam Phillips' boys too. Adrian would tilt his chin down on his chest and take deep breaths, singing with Johnny Cash. He'd beat the steering wheel with Jerry Lee, and if the drive was at night, you could see him taking private moments with Patsy Cline.

Being drunk, it was easy to call up all those memories. In his blur, he could see them from another angle, which always made him feel like he was getting something done. The uneasy feeling that makes a person do things like leave a dinner party and wander down the hill was only getting worse.

His wife, like any good liar, knew a lie a mile away. Constantly changing stories, going over old evidence, taking depositions, asking trick questions, and generally living each moment together in dread and resentment. They were locked in a struggle that knew no peace and gave no quarter. It was all about pain now. He knew she'd figure he had a woman on the phone or was meeting one someplace. He knew she'd never believe he was walking around the railroad tracks. He looked forward to being able to tell her a reason that was based on the truth. The self-righteousness would feel good for a change. It didn't matter if she believed him or not.

He was on a mission to the train yard, hoping he'd hear the seminal sound of American rock and roll. A moment of ecstasy was waiting in the dark when those railroad cars rattled and clacked past. A beat fathering the bass line used by all those pointy-shoed, longhaired, duck-butted squawlers who played out their lives in halls, clubs, barns, hayrides, tents, and on frying stages out in the clearing at county fairs. All those songs Uncle Adrian knew by heart.

Those songs he said were little lessons in life. Warnings on what to expect from the human condition.

Words sung over the mathematics of music, making life a series of hints and equations. The addition of this loss, subtracted from that gain, the sum never making sense, the answer always wrong. Like standing next to these tracks. Waiting for the train to tell him if the culture that surrounded him really came from trains. If rock and roll, besides fucking in the shanty, also had something to do with leaving.

Eyes closed, he approached the coming train, his boot tips butted up against the wooden tie. He smiled. There it was, the clackety bounce pulling him along the steel black path, promising him something better. Urging him to change everything, himself, the place he laid his head, the food he spooned in his mouth, the dog in the back yard, the shoes under the bed. Change it all, take himself somewhere else and see if he didn't like it better.

The train passed, leaving him with the memories of a hundred songs. Hearing his uncle's voice. Remembering one time when the whole clan went down to Mexico.

He was eleven, trying to laugh along with the wry wit and irony that his uncle's songs seemed to contain. But when you're eleven, you don't see the humor in things like lost love and crazy consequences. You see your mother crying and your father slamming the door. You get up late at night and one of them is in the front room sitting in the dark waiting for the other one to come home. And they don't. The house stays empty forever. Your love for them is beyond words; it runs the border of the unfathomable. You don't have a grasp of time or a lick of the good sense a man or woman needs to take care of themselves in that bedroom, in those hushed phone calls, in those chance meetings, in those second glances, in those strange smiles that Momma wouldn't like. It hurts. All that expectation, all that desire, and nowhere to go. Just something whispering that the whole world is in your young heart. But you stand there empty-handed, listening to someone fighting off tears, telling you to go back to bed.

Sixty miles south of the Mexican border, down the coastline are a series of volcanic cliffs. Black protrusions jutting out into the Pacific. At one place, two fingers point out one hundred yards and the swells surge into the palm, exploding against its jagged edges. Geysers of salt rain and torn seaweed launch with a horrifying gulp and roar, beyond and above the expectation of any boy standing under the chilling mist, shivering as the echo rolls past him back out to sea.

Uncle Adrian watches him scrambling over the tide pools, running barefoot over the volcanic mass, his feet nicked and bleeding. The rangy man stands wondering why his nephew has nothing consistent in his behavior. He raves and screams, stumbling along the ridges in one moment, then sits staring at the sky for hours. He has tried to settle the boy down, tried to find a way to communicate. Everyone has taken their turn, and the response is shrugged shoulders and raised eyebrows. From day one, he's been a weird kid. No one in the family can relate to him. He walks over to hear what the boy is saying, but it's a song he is singing to himself.

The swells begin to come in thick walls. A huge wave blasts into spray above them, coming in like silent rushing trains, carrying secrets. The boy watching, wanting something, from somewhere.

The uncle takes it on himself. He reaches back to another coast, in another world, and thinks about what he needed most and when he needed it.

Geysers pocked the shore's surface, whizzing shrapnel exploding the air around him. GI's vomit on each other as the landing craft's hull makes its walloping journey through artillery shells, to a beach. Spitting them out, to race through this metal rain. Strange popping sounds dropping farmboys like himself into the shallows. Running over men floating face down. Hitting the sand, weaving into a nightmare that stops them open-mouthed in wonder.

Huddled together, faces white with fear, certain of absolutely nothing at all, wanting only to get out alive. One by one, he watched the boys beside him fall, until he dropped and watched his fingers tremble before his eyes. So he crawled and waited. A soldier beside him had assumed the posture of one of the dead. Lying on his back with his face twisted, staring at Adrian. Managing to get his attention with the desperation in his eyes. The soldier's eyes looked upward toward the beach, then they stared at Adrian again. Then he understood the strategy. Wait until the next wave hits the beach and move forward when the machine guns strafe the troops behind them to pieces. He waited.

Large guns opened up, their explosions hitting the beach behind him. The machine guns clattered before him, their aim over his head. The screaming behind him was incessant. He crawled. The soldier flew up as though an invisible hand had grabbed the front of his helmet and pulled him toward his feet. The boy dropped, the sand yellow and red above his neck. Adrian crawled under a cement bunker, heard panic in the voices inside. Tossed in a thudding explosion and then another. He made his way to the back hatch. A torso twitched in the doorway. He waited by the body watching his sergeant lead up eight men. They stayed protected by the concrete while the war wailed past them. They waited all night, and the others told him what he had done.

He thought again of the soldier who made him wait there in the sand. What would he doing now? Adrian was on the other side of the world vacationing with his brother's family, wondering how to reach a nephew he felt was becoming more distant with every passing hour. The soldier forever in a cemetery in Italy.

Earlier that morning he stood leaning into his camper shell, rank with the smell of salt-caked, drying starfish. He reached for the burlap sack and found Eddie's collection, stiffened in asymmetrical twists, some gripping the rough brown edges of the bag, some on one another. Sad remembrances... misplaced, forgotten, dead. Adrian wondering, "*Where do we learn about life?*"

The boy sits, watching enormous silence roll below, rush past and explode above him. On the slick black surface, near kelp and seaweed, clings a huge red starfish. It appears for a second and then is submerged as the next wave rolls over. The boy stands peering down, anxious for the next glimpse of that beautiful and now impossibly treasured starfish.

His uncle appears over his shoulder.

"You want to get it?"

The boy freezes. The air pounds with the latest and largest swell; the geyser lingers above them. The boy shouts in the rain, above the roar.

"Yeah."

And then in the silence of the next wall looming toward them.

"But it's too far away."

"I'll lower you down between the waves."

The boy can't stay in the gaze of that challenge. His eyes look down into the chasm. It's a challenge coming from a kind man. A challenge alone can be answered either way. Kindness combined with challenge has to be accepted.

Adrian looks at the boy and imagines the surging wall yanking Eddie from his grasp, taking him for a long subsurface journey beneath the enormous surf into the black rocks. He sees himself leaping into the darkening sea, failing against the mountains rising, tossing him with the boy's frail blue broken body. He weighed this against the boy's burlap sack.

"If you miss... "

"I won't miss."

"Ok, then."

The boy squats down next to the man. He looks beyond the ledge and sees the dark mound rising toward him. He listens intently as his uncle explains that after the wave breaks, and the backwash surges past, he will have his ankles in his hands and drop him down into the emptying hole.

"Let's count."

After six, right between seven, the sea rushes back in, and by eight it explodes against the wall.

"I'll be dropping you on one. You'll be down there on two..."

Another larger swell rises and nearly overflows the edge.

"By five, I'll be pulling you up."

The air explodes, an avalanche of solid water douses them, filling the small pocked holes with white water and foam.

"We really gonna do this?"

"Yeah."

"Ok, then."

"Next one, see the starfish?"

The boy looks down to see the red giant.

"Yeah."

He isn't heard as a wave blasts high on the rocks and sends the next shower down on them. It suddenly seems so much darker. The backwash bounces beneath them. The boy scrambles into position. His uncle's vice-like grip hurts. The boy rolls over the side and drops for a second that stops his heart. The boy lands hard against the cold kelp lining the inside of the wash. The starfish glistens a foot beyond his grasp. The boy stretches, hearing his uncle's count of two. Out of the corner of his eye, he sees the surging tide rising above him, a black rolling wall racing in, rumbling at his intrusion.

The boy touches the starfish, his hand on the rough contour of its back. The animal is much bigger than he thought, larger than both his hands together which now pull against its grip on the rock wall. His uncle bellows four. The starfish starts to release. The boy feels his light weight raising and the wall of murky water looming above him. The heels of his hands fight for ledges to push upward, aiding the speed of his ascent. Fingernails tear into his back under his bathing suit as he feels himself yanked onto the rock edge, his one trailing arm submerged up to his shoulder under the surface as it rushes past.

"I can get it."

"Ok, then."

They turn together to face the next wave. The backwash swirls past. His ankles are again in the vice-hands of the uncle. The boy drops, bracing his fall with an outstretched arm. He bounces from the kelp wall, his eyes focused on the starfish, and he twists his return to land beside it. The fingers of both hands slipped under the edge of two legs and pry the starfish loose. He hears his uncle counting three and the sound of fear in his voice. He shoots a glance at the oncoming wall. The starfish hangs in the boy's outstretched hands.

"I got it!!"

He realizes he can not help the climb back up and hold the starfish at the same time. He feels his body begin to rise slower than it had the first time. The wall of water bearing down.

The boy blows his breath out and takes a huge lung full of air. He feels the hand dig viciously into his back, desperately pulling. His ribs catch the edge of the rocks and a sharp line of skin tears over his bony chest. An arm surrounds him and pulls him from the edge, rolling him over onto the sharp tide pool edges. The entire space swells with a foot of water. The crash against the rocks sends backwash rolling over them, the uncle clutching the boy, the boy clutching the starfish. The water recedes. They get to their feet.

Eddie holds the red starfish the size of a hubcap in his hands. His uncle looks down at it and whistles. "That's a beauty," he says. The boy spins it over an oncoming wave, watching it fade from the surface and disappear.

Adrian turns and walks back toward the International. Eddie follows him at a distance, and then runs until he catches up. They walk hand-in-hand until they see a narrow path leading them to a cliff. Adrian sweeps his arm from the ground to the cliff edge above.

"Lead the way."

Eddie runs along the cliff wall, dodging cactus, tufts of grass, his feet dislodging volcanic debris, sending stones bouncing over the side and falling into the surf. When he reaches the top, he looks down at his uncle slowly rocking his long strides up the incline. Eddie stands as close as he dares to the cliff edge and closes his eyes. He thinks he feels himself falling forward. He feels his balance adjust and doubt thrills him. He smiles to himself.

"*I'm not gonna fall.*"

He opens his eyes and looks down, yelling, "C'mon Uncle Adrian!"

The old truck always takes a few tries before starting. Adrian lights a cigarette and stretches his arm along the top of the front seat. He squints through smoke and coughs.

"Eddie, you were born in June, huh?"

Eddie nods. "The eleventh."

Adrian repeats the date. "June the eleventh. And you're eleven, ain't ya?"

Eddie nods.

Adrian pauses and stares through the windshield in concentration, exhaling little clouds.

"Well, see there? Hank Williams made his debut on the Grand Ol' Opry on the day you were born."

Adrian tries the ignition again. The engine turns over and dies.

"First time he sang 'Lovesick Blues'. Goes like this..."

Adrian takes a deep breath, twists the ignition. The truck rumbles and he sings as though he was standing at the back in tent at the country fair.

"*Ah got a feeling called the bluuuees, oh Lord since my baby said goodbye, I don't what I'll doooo...* "

He thumps the steering wheel in time.

"*All do is sit and cryyy, oh lord, I got so used to her somehow...*"

He licks his lips, looks out the side window and puts the truck in gear.

"Or something like that."

CLEANLINESS IS NEXT TO...

My father's destroyer was due to return to San Diego from a nine month Cold War cruise. Postcards, letters meaning very little, sent home. Mother always counting the days, then crying herself to sleep when he left again, and me wondering why. They never treated each other like anything but distant uncomfortable relatives after his first few days home. Awful awkward silences during television commercials. I'd do annoying things to break the tension and was usually spoken to harshly by both of them. Making them agree on something. I missed him. I missed something he was supposed to provide and the fact that I didn't know what that was made the longing greater.

We waited on the dock. The sun was shining bright and my mother was drinking coffee from a dock canteen, sharing a powdered donut with me provided by the USO cart making its way up and down the dock. We saw the USS Isherwood pass the line of silent ships at mooring. My heart jumped and we waved at the sailors in formation standing on the deck of the ship in the distance. Minutes crawled as the ship made its way to the pier and shaded us in its shadow. Piping whistles, thrown lanyards, horns, and the ship's band playing the Navy Hymn. I saw my father walking above us along the cable barriers on the edge of the deck. I could recognize his walk anywhere. My mother intoning, "There he is." We waved as his back dressed in blues and his Chief's hat disappeared into a hatch.

The plank was lowered and the crowd of dependents moved up the plank and onto the ship's deck to hug and kiss their men, sobbing smiles, introducing babies. Solemn handshakes from boys to fathers. Down the gray ladders, down the gray halls and into the Chief's quarters. Finally released, my father was permitted to leave ship and return with us to our house for a few months until the next cruise would take him around the world.

My father at the wheel of the Oldsmobile and my mother turned toward him in the front seat speaking about details of life beyond the scope of a third grade boy just happy to smell the diesel on his clothes. The smell of manhood.

Then the hours changed to days and the monotony got to my father, bringing back the tension, which eventually drifted downward toward me. My father tried to reestablish his fatherhood by using discipline. I wanted to be taken in his lap and held, lifted into the air, taken on walks. Invited into the garage to smell the wood burn on his table saw, watch the spinning blade whirl near his thick skillful fingers. Instead, I played down the street and left him alone with his depression and his boredom. Conversations about trespasses I'd committed in the days of his absence led to lectures and punishments. Reduced television privileges. Boring busywork after school. Disappointed looks directed at a sailor of nine who was not making the grade.

My mother and father sat stunned in catatonic silence watching the fourth steady hour of regular television programming. I wandered from the cupboard holding a handful of Oreos and an orange. I laid down on the floor under the blue television light and was thereby noticed by my father.

"Go take a bath."

Just that. Deadpan.

I kept my eye on the screen and said, "No."

Silence. The mindless dialogue droned on the set.

"I'm not going to tell you again. Take a bath."

"No."

My mother made an unintelligible noise of protest, a groan or something. My father wasted no time.

"Go get a belt."

I stuffed another Oreo in my mouth and walked past the stares coming from the couch. I turned on the light in their bedroom and opened his dresser drawer. Pulled out a plastic braided belt I'd made for him when he was overseas. I walked out into the front room and held it out to him.

My legs were bare. He went for them. He swung hard enough to count but not really committed to damage or to venting his anger. The sound wasn't too impressive, but it hurt like hell. He waited. He hit me again. I gained some kind of strength from it and I knew I'd be ok. He shook his head like a television character about to shrug off some homily. But he didn't say anything. He hit me instead. I thought how stupid he was not to know that my leg was getting numb. He was really getting upset.

"Get your ass into the bathtub or..."

He hit me in the other leg, let it glide past me and backhanded me on the other. He did it again. The pain was constant and harder to stand. I got a little scared that I wouldn't be able to hold on. But his eyes were tearing up, and he was losing heart. He hit me again. My mother said that I was bleeding. I was crying on the outside, but not on the inside. His shoulders sagged. His hand dropped to his side. His eyes were full of tears. My voice sounded so calm it startled me.

"I already took a bath."

MY DAD CURED ME OF GUNS

Christmas at the Mexican-American border usually brings a heat wave. The temperature peaks around one o'clock at ninety degrees. The sunlight is bright and the air is crisp; it's absolutely beautiful, shining and clear. The air shimmers. The winter sun doesn't burn; it blesses.

Waking up in the early morning, Eddie examines what is wrapped for him under the tree. Being eleven, he is in the limbo years of his youth. Between the playground and his first car, the no-girls-allowed-club and his first crush. His place in the future is a source of anxiety. Who is he? Who will he become? Is there a way to effect the outcome? His assessment of who he is today is embarrassing. He is tired of childhood. Next spring, he wants a spot on the baseball team; to find out if he can hit the curve, take one for the team, hang in there, play the field, get low on the ball, steal second and prove that he has what it takes to become a teenager. Right now, any thirteen year-old could easily bulldoze his life.

One present has a note written in his father's formal hand. Lifting the package, its weight and density triggers his curiosity. The other presents under the tree lift easily. They rattle; they lack dignity. Presents probably containing toys and games that will prove his parents still regard him today as the child he was last month.

Eddie's father and mother have taken their place on the couch. Eddie opens the front door and sunlight streams through and leaves the faintest trace of tiny squares on the floor. A sunlight so bright, sharp, and clear that it seems like music. His father clears his throat. Eddie turns, watching his mother stretch and yawn behind one hand.

"Let's open them presents."

Eddie stands looking at these familiar strangers. Two middle-aged figures slumped beside each other like Martians, a canyon of alienation between them. The distance between the man in his boxers and the woman in her robe so vast that she begins to hug herself as though she were cold. Eddie walks to the Christmas tree.

"I been wondering what could it be that was in here."

His father fixes him with a mocking challenge.

"Well, then you better open it and see."

His father takes his mother's hand. She shifts uneasily.

The present is even heavier than he remembered. Something in it makes him open it slowly. He's eleven; he doesn't just rip the paper anymore.

"Read the card, Eddie." Her voice is admonishing.

"I did. Says 'To Eddie, Christmas 1960.'"

The cardboard box is open at one end and the blond stock, blue-grey barrel and bolt of a Remington .22 Savage slides slowly onto the carpet. Astonished, Eddie looks at his father. His large arms are folded against his chest; his mother's abandoned hand trails absently through his long black hair and down his neck to rest on his shoulder. He takes on something more manly than Eddie has seen in him before. A look as though he were letting him into the clubhouse. A reassuring smile that could be saying:

"Had you worried there for a while. Didn't know where ya stood didja? Welcome to the first stair to the man's world, kid. Ya made it."

She seems pleased and tries to participate in the admiration of the weapon, but her comments are drowned in the solemn instructions of gun safety as the weapon is assembled.

Eddie is over-attentive and over-respectful, feeling phony, but the strange occasion carries such weight and is so reverent that the delirium of this new passage forgives his corny effort at maturity. He can almost hear the theme from Bonanza playing in the front room; Pa intoning in serious sermon the principles of men. His father standing with feet wide as a cop's, assembling the rifle, breaking it down.

"Now you do it, Son."

Eddie frozen, the gun offered in his father's outstretched hand. Eddie thinking, *"He's never called me Son."*

He takes the bolt, sets it on the table, places the barrel beside it, takes the stock and fits the barrel to it. His hands shake. He waits for his father's humiliating comment. But he remains silent while Eddie fits the bolt to the barrel.

His father gets up for a refill. Eddie's mother hands him another present. A black mohair sweater with athletic stripes at the biceps. Perfect. She opens the photo album. His father returns with the coffee and opens the series of blades and bits for his power tools— neither gift a surprise, both of them acting as though it were. The room opening into a chasm of lonely phoniness that years of practice has made excusable.

Christmas 1960 passes through the crucial phase. No one has broken the suspension of disbelief. Cheeks are kissed, thank yous are muttered, embarrassments are left unexposed. Eddie's father heads for the bathroom. His mother begins pressing the wrapping paper into neat folds to be put away to wrap presents next year. Eddie heads out the screen door.

The sun amplifies the greens, golds, and blues outside. Everything shines. Eddie walks barefoot in the cool grass, the sun warm on his back. The street is silent. Birds swoop to the wires hanging over the house, change their mind and settle in the jacaranda tree across the street. A neighborhood girl flies past, her chin over her handlebars, her legs motionless, having pedaled as fast as her Schwinn's gear will torque. Her hair streaming behind her, face ecstatic. Eddie whistles through his teeth and her hand waves behind her, the spokes of her bike glistening.

Eddie walks into the front room. His mother is on the phone checking in with relatives, feigning interest in each other's gifts and in the dinner plans for later.

Eddie stands there watching. His mother taps ashes into last year's present, nodding on the phone, already bored with her call.

Eddie can never locate reality. It keeps slipping into these deceptions between all of the people he lives with. No one tells the truth. Television means more than any of his close relatives. Conversation means nothing; affection is forced and painful. No spirit, no soul, no pride anywhere. And where is the appropriate place to deposit this anger? On the woman on the couch, pretending she cares about the next twenty-four hours? Is she so stupid she can't see that she is slaving for a son and husband who can't see her? What can his father do but go to sea, take orders, come home, and wait to ship out again? What does this make Eddie? Eddie does not want to answer that question yet. He does what he always does—watches them and stalls for time.

Eddie knows this Christmas was intended as a rite of passage. He walks into his bedroom. It has changed. The rocket ship wallpaper is childish. The toys are embarrassing. He has a gun.

The water's running in the bathroom sink. His father leans into the mirror examining his neck and tapping the whiskers from his razor. His words are distorted as he cuts the stubble on the side of his mouth. He asks if Eddie would like to take the gun out into the canyon.

"Yes, sir."

Eddie never calls him sir.

They're walking along a dirt road that's twenty minutes by truck from the house. His father pulls a box of shells from his jacket. Eddie carries the rifle in the crook of his arm, balancing it like a television mountain man. He lowers his voice when he speaks, struggling to deepen it within his rib cage. They walk along, talking in mature, slow tones, struggling for subjects worthy of manly discourse. Not much to say. They fall in the gulf of father-son relationship. They slip a .22 Long into the bolt. Eddie is taught to squeeze the trigger at beer cans. In a few minutes, they spin under the impact of newfound ballistic acumen. Eddie examines the holes tearing through the metal. He struggles to find some noble imagery. Frontiersmen bring home food for the young. A Bud can is the sternum of a bear, pawing the air in his last seconds of agony. Eddie's friends behind him, reloading after their panicked shots have missed; him saving them from the giant clubbing claws.

Eddie's father sights and shoots. Reloads, shoots, reloads, shoots. His smile is bitter as the last shot slams into the dirt. Eddie cannot find a disarming comment to ease his father's embarrassment.

Slipping another bullet into the bolt, his father is muttering.

"Rusty cans don't mean shit."

Eddie follows his father beneath brush and tangled sycamore. His father's tattooed hand parts a green sunlight speckled branch. A blue jay nods, bright-eyed, head tilting, wings ruffled and shaking back into place. The barrel levels and Eddie's father's jaw sets, his eye widens, his breath stops. He squeezes the trigger.

"Merry Christmas bird."

POST PERFORMANCE

A train robber and a fourteen year-old girl are left following an unsuccessful attempt at stopping a train. The horses wheeled, the guns fired, bullets whizzed, a few of them splattered through men intent on defending or stealing money. It ended five minutes ago. The girl and the thief remain in the aftermath.

She sees his torn, dusty jeans, dried sweat, dirt encrusted, hollow-eyed exhaustion. He is high on adrenaline and the euphoria of escaping death. His bleeding cracked lips are smiling. There is no skin on his right forearm, shoulder and hip. There's a blue knot on the side of his head; bramble has torn an ear. His canteen is three-quarters empty. They are thirty-seven miles from bath, food, lace curtains, and a wide bed where his woman turns over on her hip sleeping deeply, dreaming of canyons in shade and fire running their ridges. He looks at the girl. The first words out of his mouth are an excuse, or an explanation. In either case, she will miss the point.

"So, when they sold the farm out from under us... and didn't compensate us, other than to remind us of our poverty... I got pissed."

He shrugs, offering her the last of the canteen, which she appreciates since she is thirsty as hell, and has had more than her share already. He looks away, saying wordlessly that he expects her to finish it.

"And you know, it feels real good to be an outlaw. To stand exactly in the square of slings and arrows, and directly in the path of outrageous fortune."

He laughs at himself. Remembering Lilly Langtree.

She is stunned hearing Shakespeare quoted out here in the duststorm that is picking up around them. When she left St. Louis, she thought it would be an adventure and here it is standing in front of her—a coarse man limping off an injured hip, flourishing his words by throwing his arms in the air.

He waves his hand in the direction of his lost land, and the empty railroad tracks where an hour ago was the stage of life and death.

He pulls some of the worn shirt off the raw skin of his shoulder. Tears fill his eyes and he winces, which surprises her since she thought he'd make a show of being brave. He squints down at her.

"Next time, I won't bother to wear a kerchief over my face..."

She doubts that he'll have to.

He clomps around in his boots; one heel is broken off. He pitches to the side with each stride. He pulls off his boots. He walks over to a ditch where most of the shooting came from, and comes back wearing someone else's. She hasn't moved a muscle. Sweat is running down her face, her hat has nearly blown off in the wind. He mops her face with his kerchief and hands it to her. She tucks it between her breasts. He is oblivious.

"It's a damn sad day when you have to shoot your own horse. Well, it's a long walk, so I guess we'd better get started."

They begin to walk at right angles from the railroad tracks.

"You don't talk much, do you?"

The girl just shakes her head.

RITA

ASummer of 1964 was a heat wave blowing over flaming cities, police dogs, draft induction centers, universities, prisons, self-immolating monks, civil rights workers deep in the slave states, and San Diego asleep on the Mexican border.

Eddie Burnett's relatives are visiting from Chicago. Over the past months, his mother, father, uncle, aunt and three cousins have driven up the coast to Seattle and seen the Space Needle. Gone to Disneyland, driven to Marineland, hit Knott's Berry Farm on one of the smoggiest days in Los Angeles history, and spent the last month hanging around the house.

Because of his father's flatulence, and the weird squawking whine that his mother has developed, each undoubtedly a form of passive aggression designed to avoid proximity with the relatives, the inter-family trips have come to a halt. The summer vacation was planned to last until August, and last it will, even if the meals are eaten separately, or in resentful silence.

Eddie's aunt and uncle are early risers. They read the paper first, pissing off his mother who likes to get it fresh off the lawn and read it without egg and coffee stains. The aunt takes long showers, using most of the hot water. The deaf uncle follows her, singing to the top of his lungs. Show tunes waking the rest of the family who fight for the remaining hot water.

Around ten o'clock Eddie's mother grinds her toast into a paste by chewing it hundreds of times, annoying all hell out of the cousins, who are slurping cereal and making jokes at Eddie's expense. They like to make him spell words, and laugh hysterically when he fails to get them right. Eddie opens a can of fruit cocktail and swallows it in four non-stop gulps. He disappears out the screen door, leaving his cousins to hang around the house while the bickering adults shift from one room to the other, whispering shit about each other.

But the next day is Eddie's fourteenth birthday, and to celebrate everybody is going to the zoo. By seven o'clock both families are clogging the door to the bathroom, bumping into each other in the kitchen, and yelling at the kids. The race to be ready first begins with Eddie's aunt pointing out that, judging from the amount of fruit salad Eddie's father had last night, it might be best to take separate cars. Eddie's mother takes her sister to the side and whines that this teasing about a little fart now and then has gotten out of hand. Eddie's uncle has the TV cranked up to maximum, listening to the morning news, announcing at the top of his lungs that there won't be any rain today. Eddie mumbles that he doubts that it will since it's already one hundred and two degrees, and there ain't a cloud in the goddamn sky. The biggest cousin tells Eddie to watch his wise-guy mouth and Eddie suggests that he fuck himself. This of course, gets the feathers flying, ending with a broken chair and both women running to separate rooms to cry over it.

Eddie's inability to follow simple instructions costs his racing parents too much time in the contest to be ready to leave first. Eddie's family's efforts are regarded with disgusted snorts from his aunt's family, who stand beside their car and wait patiently for the less competent Burnetts to finally get ready.

Eddie's aunt barks, "Eddie, front and center!"

This she expects will elicit the same response it does in her own sons, or maybe it's meant to demonstrate the hopeless state of discipline in her sister's boy. In any case, Eddie does not make it front or center. He makes it out the door and down the street, yelling honk when you're ready to leave.

By noon on one of the hottest days in San Diego history, Eddie and his father are sitting on a bench under the trees that shade the largest collection of primates in the world. Seventy cages of varying species, all of them clearly out of their minds, imprisoned in hot-boxes, and fed up with another season of peanut-tossing tourists. Ambulances are wailing in and out of the parking lot treating twenty sun stroke victims an hour. Thousands of sunburns are already lobster-red heading toward purple. The heat is driving everyone into delirium. An old man standing near Eddie's father has eyes that sit back in his head like a cadaver's. His face is red wax. His tiny wife's old ankles are swollen over her shoes; her mouth is open and she is panting. Eddie whispers they should give up their seats to the elderly couple before they collapse. As they stand, two high school girls pretend to be oblivious and sit down. The old couple shuffles off in the direction of Deer Canyon. Eddie and his father join the mindless amble of exhausted and suffering vacationers milling past a row of monkey cages.

Monkey eyes follow Eddie. There is not a single primate looking anywhere except directly into Eddie's eyes. Each face frozen in disbelief. Time stops. No one breathes, no hearts beat, there are no birds in flight, no one speaks, the heat is gone. The entire zoo hovers in a vacuum. The bars are optical illusions. We are caged in our mindless condescension. They are crucified. They understand everything we are doing to them. Eddie becomes terrified.

A single wild cry unleashes a chorus of slanders and shrieks. Gibbons scramble up the cage screen, stabbing their arms out of the wire mesh at Eddie. The shrieking does not decrease as he passes.

Wires shake in fists, eyes roll white, leaping figures fly from floor to ceiling, banging full speed into the fences between Eddie and these homicidal creatures.

Seventy monkey cages are in full riot. Suspicious attendants begin to arrive. People are muttering, pointing out Eddie who must have somehow tormented these chimpanzees rolling drunk with rage on their deck, arms flailing, gibbons unhinged jaws snapping spike teeth, spider monkeys gnashing and whizzing above him. The shrieks engulf and shame him. He decides to find a place to retreat. He looks back toward his father who is laughing, convulsing on a bench holding his stomach yelling, "Hey, Eddie, where ya going? Where ya going? Eddie?"

Eddie heads down to Deer Canyon, which is an inferno without shade. The asphalt road mushes under his feet. There is no breeze. A tour group trudges up the hill, each tented under a canopy of newspaper. An attendant with a walkie-talkie is leading the old couple toward a curb. Eddie plunges down into the canyon. People coming up are gasping things at him.

"Don't go down there."

"Too hot, go back."

Eddie picks up a discarded newspaper, places his head in the fold and disappears down the hillside.

For the next two hours, Eddie stays near a drinking fountain watching a cape buffalo frothing in a cloud of flies. When the setting sun leaves the canyon shaded near closing time, Eddie, with nothing else to do, reads the paper. A church was bombed in Birmingham. A bible class of kids his own age were blown up. Four little girls died. After the third loudspeaker announces the final call before closing, Eddie sneaks up to the baboon cage.

He holds his eyes down. Sliding over the rail, he crouches against the screen. A guy with a broom ten cages down is sweeping slowly.

A huge graying male leads an ancient female's approach. She sits turning her back. The male watches the guy sweeping. The old matriarch turns her head.

He waits, expecting a sign, looking for some kind of answer. Her bloodshot eye slides slowly over his face. Knuckles whack the concrete floor. Callused lips pull up, revealing black gums and the top quarter of huge yellow teeth. A nostril cave blows wet hot gusts on Eddie's cheek. Her face recomposes without a trace of anything from this millennia.

The snoring and the musings of apes asleep buzzes low in the late afternoon heat. She stretches and lumbers away. The male follows her, looking backward over his shoulder on every other stride.

"What the hell are you doing? Goddamn it, we been waiting an hour."

Eddie is marched out of the zoo, across the parking lot and thrown into the Oldsmobile. They leave the park and drive home.

Eddie looks through the back seat window. Time stops again.

A church. A neon sign glows *Jesus is Love.* A fireball blows down the church's front door. The explosion lifting him out of the back seat, his head thuds on the car roof. His father asks him what the hell is going on. Then everything returns as it was.

Eddie mumbles.

"Don't mumble."

"Where's Birmingham?"

"What?"

"Nothing."

"Birmingham is in England. Don't they teach ya nothing in school?"

"Oh."

"Dad, everything is really a war isn't it?"

"What?"

"Everything is a war."

"Ah, yeah, I guess so."

"I mean everybody is against everybody else, right?"

"Uh, huh."

Eddie's mother says, "That's not true, honey."

Eddie's father waits at a long stoplight.

"You shoulda seen those monkeys screaming at Eddie."

"What?"

"When we were down at the monkey cage. Shoulda seen 'em. Right Eddie?"

"Yeah."

"What do you guys want for dinner?"

"I dunno."

"I dunno. Hey, Dad, ya know they bombed a church in Birmingham."

"They did?"

"Yeah."

"Hmmm. Too bad."

Two thousand miles away, Rita sat over the wing watching the green land below, the intermittent flashes as the setting sun bounced off the web of the Mississippi's tributaries. Nothing registered. Fatigue and fear had disembodied her. The plane dropped, the airfield below rose, the tires bumped, the plane taxied toward a little tower with a small cafe beside it. She watched the blurring circle beside her.

A low cyclone fence in front of the cafe bore the weight of three baggy-suited photographers, each with a jacket in the crook of an elbow—sunglasses, white cotton shirts, loosened ties, and expressions on their tanned faces that seemed to know plenty. Tight thin lipped mouths that said little. They were blurred in the rippling heat like three emissaries from hell, moving toward the shade under the wing of the airplane.

The doors opened. The windows steamed over; Rita's clothes

stuck to her skin. The other passengers waved newspapers under their chins. Her suitcase weighed a ton and bounced off her knee as she descended the stairs. A knot of reporters and onlookers waited.

Microphones obscured her vision as she tried to walk. She searched the crowd, hoping someone would shout over the mob of reporters, policemen, and gawkers.

"He's alive! Turned up five hours ago!"

There was no voice. Just the mumbling of the reporters and Klansmen like gravel rolling underwater. She strode on saying nothing to the increasingly demanding questions. A loud snarl.

"Why are you here?"

She searched the men towering over her until she located the eyes laughing at her. He continued.

"The best place for you is right back where you came from... and the best place for your husband is right where he is."

Eyes shifted from Rita to the voice shuffling through the crowd as it parted for him. The eyes slowly revolved back to her and waited for a response.

"I am here to find out who killed my husband. The best place for anyone to be who knows anything about the whereabouts of my husband, or anything pertaining his disappearance, is on the phone with the Attorney General of the United States. I have been promised an FBI investigation beginning tomorrow morning."

Six reporters turned and ran for the telephone hanging on the wall inside the airport. The FBI... here. Any fool could see a Commie troublemaker happened to fall into the wrong hands.

"And if you people don't like it, you can go ahead and kill me just like you killed my husband."

Nothing moved, until the soles of shoes scratched uneasily around her. A half-circle of men stared at her, each occasionally spitting through their teeth, hands in pockets. Three in the center slowly shook their heads from side to side. One smiled broadly.

"The heat must be getting to you, Miss. Nobody wants to see anybody killed."

They turned in unison and walked toward the parking lot.

As Rita passed, a young man's voice rose in volume and screeched out of his chest.

"Excuse me, Miss.. er... Mrs.. ah... Can I say something?"

Rita kept walking.

"Does it have to do with my husband?"

"Well, ah.. yeah. It does."

Rita faced him.

"Would it help him to get yourself killed? What good would that do?"

She turned toward him. He began to sight his camera on her, his hand twisted around the lens, and then he lowered it.

She examined his face. It was self-conscious, ashamed. From head to toe, a tall, rumpled, chinless wonder, lost, scared, and ignorant. His face reminding her of her mother telling her to stay home; her father, resigned, turning slowly from the front porch to the screen door.

She did not really hear the young man explaining that she was only falling right into the Klan's hands, that she didn't understand how it was down here.

Her words fell out so weary and sad.

"I don't think you understand."

She walked past the staring faces and found a booth in a tiny coffee shop.

The photographer stood in the doorway changing cameras, hoping for a shot before she left for her probable appointment in some ditch by the side of the road.

He noticed his hands shaking and realized he was afraid she'd see him and address him, confront him and tell him more things about himself that he wouldn't understand. He began to hate her.

Rita crossed her arms, turned her head and stared straight at him as he found her in his camera. He lowered it, raised his eyes and saw her smile faintly, the slightest softening in her face, and the smallest movement of her mouth.

She turned her hipster sunglassed gaze toward the telephone on the wall. One hand rose slowly, her thumb rubbed her bottom lip then it folded into a small relaxed fist, and froze. The camera clicked. Rita stared into eternity.

5-28-92

That loud clean snap means a sharp blade. One that leaves you staggering and aching from lack of blood before you can judge the depth of the slice.

But a serrated edge tears a rip that lets you assess the depth, the speed and the damage, via an unforgiving pain. The ragged edge sawing past skin that yearned for more kinds of living than minutes provide, pulling through muscle made weak in the refusal to take less than the treasures laid at my feet. Stopping me in my tracks, asleep at the wheel, under the influence of fits of euphoria producing nothing but insight, turning to hindsight, mocking me as time moved on.

That was the sin that made those angels groan. Made them turn their faces and sing in tongues that I couldn't understand but had that simple refrain, about living only once and the time is running out. Just barely long enough to fit in one more promise.

The edge tears more than it cuts. The surface just broken, then torn gashing to the bone. Past skin slick with kisses, wet with the abor life requires, rivulets of saline rolling down the cheek now vening in a red instant. The vicious need we have to work each other over into something we think we want, but don't know what to do with when it faces us.

Our shadows fade in the light; our tired eyes grow weak. We jinx ourselves muttering, "What's the use?"

We stare, recognizing a curse when we utter one.

Because we need it all. And that bus left a long time ago and it's only the echo of its gears grinding around the turn we hear, making us believe we can catch up. So we wait there alone in the dark. Crickets sounding invitations to a warm night, breeze blowing in a way we think we remember, stars above us like a map we can't read, newspapers sliding around us like snakes in the air. Waiting.

Transforming in the dark, she is a dervish dancing and singing that she loves me, or what I was, or what I once imagined myself to be. Becoming a blur, whirling and pulling a bent steak knife, hissing, "Here. I'll give you something to remember me by."

TRIP THE LIGHT FANTASTIC

Don't ask me how long this'll take. I don't have a fucking idea. If I did then I'd be done with it already because the reason it isn't done is because it's gonna be fucked and I can't stand the idea of getting started, and then you know, having to go on and on and on with all the shit that goes with it. Anyway, I gotta wait here for a minute more, the fuck will be coming back to his car any second. Meanwhile, I gotta wait here and try to look inconspicuous. The car radio blaring, the light's on and the key's in the ignition. Is he asking me to just jump in and drive? I see his brown, shiny shoe stepping out the door, his expensive and tasteless slacks snap in the breeze. He isn't even looking where he's going. So I bump into him and he's a solid fuck; he doesn't budge. I say excuse me to throw him off, and he gives me a funny look and before he can tell me it's alright, he sees the knife in my hand and he looks at me again. I nod and hold out my hand saying something to him that I can't remember even though it just came out of my mouth. I'm scared that's why. And I hate to be scared. The guy is slow so I tell him to give me his money before I... But I just did cut him, right down his arm and I'm now punching the blade under his ribs. He's backing up and the look in his eyes tells me he's another asshole who won't go down. Fuck, I hate this. I hope he doesn't die. I hate this.

FOR THE RECORD

The Lincoln Brigade were volunteers from the United States who fought in the Spanish Civil War against the fascist forces lead by General Francisco Franco just prior to World War II. Picasso's piece "Guerneca" condemns the first use of air warfare on civilian populations by Hitler's Luftwaffe in that same war.

The Spanish Civil War was a slaughter in which another chip of mankind's collective soul was lost. A war where Germany tested its Twentieth Century weapons on cities without air raid sirens, without any means of defense, with nothing but an innocence that was left burning in rubble. The world stood back in horror, pounding pedestals, screaming protests in newspaper headlines, and waiting to see how far the Third Reich was willing to go. In the most real sense the first battles against Hitler's extermination camps were fought by men like, my friend, Bill Bailey. Communists, labor organizers, and blue collar heroes from New York's docks who were used to standing up immediately when they faced heartlessness and violence rained on innocent women and children. They formed a brigade without adequate ammunition and weapons, far outnumbered, fought in a country where they did not speak the language, understand the culture, or the terrain. They fought and they lost.

Bill Bailey is respected for his participation in that war, and in later years for his courage on the stand during the McCarthy era of political repression in the 1950's. By the time I met him he was in his seventies. His hands were the size of baseball gloves. He was tall and stooped slightly with age, his face craggy and his eyes looking sad as though he could see right through you and what he saw made him isolated, distant, alone. His manner was warm, grandfatherly. He seemed to be always on the verge of saying good-bye.

On a December in the 1980's, Bill and I sat on a bench overlooking the slate-gray San Francisco Bay. The morning overcast and cold, container ships plowing under the Golden Gate, seagulls suspended in updrafts, rush hour traffic stopped, a bakery smelling sweet to the point of nausea. The Contragate scandal was threatening to explode; we were talking about Ollie North, his connections to Reagan. I was hoping the administration would fall. But Bill shook his head saying that the government would never let an assassination be followed by a resignation be followed by impeachment inside of twenty years.

"The instability would bring the entire government down."

I was younger then. I thought at the time that a corrupt government's fall would be worth the instability. Expose the whole thing. Embrace Thomas Paine's *Common Sense*. Bill's look stopped my end-to-end sentences.

"Anarchy would be a ugly thing. It's always comes down to people. Not the people governing, but the people being governed. Right now they're too comfortable. They'd never handle it. It's easier for most of us to be exploited than it is for us to look out for each other."

I adjusted, agreeing with him. I raised the question about the CIA killing, torturing, and repressing people in our name. Bill looked out at the container ship heading for Oakland. Beneath his face I could see something hurting. He swallowed. He stood and we started walking.

I told him I thought the war raging between Iran and Iraq was the result of the United States efforts to destablize the area and keep oil prices down.

During Christmas a battle had killed thousands of kids pitted against each other by both sides. There was no sign of surrender, just climbing casualty lists. River banks piled with the bodies of wave after wave of suicide charges. Their God had assured them a spot in heaven if they'd die today. I didn't realize who I was talking to, or what it was I was evoking in his memory. I didn't care. I had theories, I needed facts. I wanted someone to make sense of it for me. Bill nodded his head with my breathless tirade.

Ten minutes later I was still at it, telling him in Honduras, American troops were poised and ready for invasion into Panama. Death squads yanked families apart, people disappeared. Central America was a war zone fought without lines, without explanation, without the slightest compassion.

I went on. The nature of fascism. The fact of it in our own governmental policies. Bill was engaged in part of the conversation when we recalled President Eisenhower's farewell to the nation in 1960, when the President admitted the existence of and warned us of the dangers of what he called, "the Military Industrial Complex." I went on to the television media discovering its power in the election of that year—Kennedy defeating Nixon by virtue his on-screen charisma. How the country became brainwashed and economics tied directly to the Pentagon had set the foundation for what was now our fascist state. He tried to tell me all these issues had a validity, that in his mind the facts supported my anger. But something kept coming through—his emphasis was on the spirit. I thought at the time it was the result of his age and his proximity to the end of his life. That somehow the years had run the urgency out of him. That he was trying to make peace with something.

"We can identify all of these things with our minds. But what it comes down to is what we feel in our hearts..."

His old hand covered his chest like a child saluting the flag.

"... how we treat each other, what we will stand for and what we won't. But people are mistrustful of what they feel these days, so we're sorta lost."

But I knew despite all of my information, what he was saying was lost. We walked on and I wondered how a person could say so much with so few words. I wanted everything I could learn from him; I was in such a hurry.

I asked him about his involvement in the war in Spain. What motivated him to risk his life for a losing cause.

"What da ya mean? Ya mean at the beginning? Ah, it was a lot of things. But I remember seeing a newsreel of a Nazi beating an old woman, and I thought, she could be my mudda."

Simple as that. Left his girl, left his job, sailed across the Atlantic, fought with strangers against strangers because a thug was filmed beating an old woman.

On our return from our walk along the bay, we stopped again at the bench we had been sitting on. I tried to explain what I thought, what I felt, in my heart. I got nowhere. The words were inadequate. Bill's gigantic face creased into a smile, his huge hand covered my shoulder and shook me gently.

"Don't despair, don't despair."

Don't despair? I could almost hear him from half a century past telling his overrun comrades, "Don't despair."

1993

Just read what the commanding officer of the United States contingent of the forces in Somalia said explaining the actions of the "Peace Keeping Mission." He admitted they killed over one hundred civilians, mostly women and children shooting them with 50mm cannons from helicopters. Said they were *combatants*. Women and children. Our enemies are women and children. Should I despair yet? Guess I'll call Bill.

1995.

When I leave, the warm bed creaks. Carmen usually sleeps late, having worked until one or two and needing another couple hours to finally settle down to sleep. She breathes where am I going? I tell her, "Coffee and the paper."

This winter it's usually raining when I make my way out to 16th Street. The car's morning headlights wink over the Mission District's streets. The slanting shower splashing sidewalks, windows, awnings, umbrellas. The asphalt is slick, black and hissing with passing car's tires.

I get the paper with the same bad news from the same girl behind the counter, get the same smile, exchange an extra sentence between us trying to make the transaction human, and then I cross the street. The dealers stare and lope around the corner like dogs. Skinny, scabby junkies bum change and crack wise with each other. Someone is always raving. The cops fly past to tape off the latest crime scene. Ambulances converge in some fixed point in the near distance.

They make a double espresso and drop it in a cup of coffee when they see me come in the door. There's a seat at a window table, I settle in. As I read, the coffee grows acidic as I grasp again, the meaning of what I am reading. All these killings, technological advances, and hype for sports and entertainment. All these personalities we are supposed to care about, the latest disaster, the coming ecological disaster. The insinuations that some countries are doomed and some aren't, the reduction of health, education and welfare. Kids killing kids makes the news, but not unless they are under eleven. Everybody pointing their fingers at everybody. Everything selling out from sea to shining sea. Movies extolling the same stupid macho garbage. Music incorporated to the point of a bad joke. Art unfunded. The mass worship of the consensus opinion. The empire in a tailspin.

An older gentleman is a fixture at the coffee shop. He looks like a Southern General. White goatee. Hair around his collar. Tall, weathered from years of sun and windburn in Minnesota. He's a translator. Worked for Army Intelligence during the early Cold War years in Germany during the occupation. He writes on a thick pad for hours, occasionally taking a smoke on the sidewalk.

We've become friends. One morning he walked to my table and identified the absurdity I was reading, which the newspaper passed off as governmental policy, as I laughed to myself. We commented to each other regarding the harshness of contemporary society, hard chic defined as the style of psychic self-defense adopted by many of the young people within the city. We wonder at what is happening to us. We dodge the topic of our fear. We omit our complicity in our community's distancing of each of us from the other. We tackle easier problems—racism, sexism, the problems of the generations misunderstanding of the view of the other, the advancement of biotechnology and the potential for disaster within its runaway acceptance and rush for product. This brave new world. This new world order. The conglomerates, the war industry. We wonder what we will tolerate from our military, what we will tolerate from the government, the Republican agenda, the Christian Right's takeover of education, the privatization of prisons and what that could mean. And we try to find our place in it. And we fail. Which is what it really comes down to. Our failure.

His father was a union activist on the railroads of the Minnesota-Canadian border. He and his father had fallen out when he was young. Never really regained the closeness they needed. Almost made it, almost understood his relationship to his father, but his father died. The rest of the family froze him out. More respectable people I guess. More in line I guess. Playing it safer I guess. Christians I guess. Good Christians I guess. We were getting nowhere, so I mentioned Bill Bailey. Of course he knows who he is. Heard his name many times. Saw the television special on him. Read his book, *Kid From Hoboken*, even. Never met him. Would like to someday. His goatee spreading over his face.

I did the normal routine the day I had to catch the plane to Florida to read from this book and be the guest of several literature and writing classes at a small university there. Thirty thousand feet over Arizona, I was reading the paper and chuckling to myself. I turned for some reason to the obituaries and there was William Bailey. A long piece revealing the modesty of the man. It was there in three long columns. He had done more, said more, seen more, and put more at stake than those of us who met him later in his life would have dreamed. He had claimed to have been in the rear for most of those losing battles in Spain, when it appeared he was never out of the action. He had admitted taking part in a demonstration in which the Nazi swastika was ripped from the flagpole and dropped into the New York harbor while the Bremen's crew and a handful of protesters fought on the deck. He hadn't said it was he who had cut it off and thrown it into the water below. Or that it had been he who his friends selected to be at the center of the flying wedge they formed to clear the way to the ship's stern. That it was he who they knew, at about amidships, would be on his own to fight his way alone to the flag, signaling the refusal of the longshoremen to off-load the Bremen's cargo in the harbor to protest the new Third Reich's persecution of Jews.

We all want to meet a giant don't we? We all want to shake hands with a hero. We mark part of our lives by the day we met someone known to be brave, human, foolish, principled, and enduring. Especially enduring. We want those people to endure for us, to be here, to never leave our side. To endure for us. To not leave us to despair in our own small lives, our own lack of what it is to be fully human. The great heroes are compassionate. Above everything, they are compassionate.

I got back from Florida. I whispered, "Coffee and the paper," to Carmen. I crossed another rainy street, bought a paper. Found a chair, drank my coffee and the older gentleman crossed the coffee shop floor to my table, bowed slowly from the waist, placed Bill's obituary before me, turned and walked away.

CRAZY HORSE

Some people say Crazy Horse got his name from a vision. His father was a Lakota shaman, a medicine man, a healer. His father was loved and respected by the tribe. His father's name was Crazy Horse and at that time his own name was Curly.

Curly was sent on a vision quest and reported the results to his elders. He'd seen a hail storm, a hawk, lightning, heard the pounding of hooves. Curly's young life was taken into account. His capacity as a provider. His adamant personality. His cool bravery. His awkward behavior during ceremonies, his reluctance to participate. Curly was a young man on the brink. He could fulfill himself, or he could destroy himself—he was walking the line. It came time to name him.

For two days and nights, the elders could not find a name to fit the odd, highly capable and troubled boy. The men waited for the name. None came. Finally Curly's father spoke.

"Curly will be called Crazy Horse. I will be known from now on as Worm."

Thanks to:
Jill Stoddard for helping to unlock the mysteries of editing. David Eggers for his illustrations. Everybody at 2-13-61 Publications. Stan Fairbank for the book design. My friends for their encouragement and interest in my writing.

My wife, Carmen and her beautiful son.

To my friend Henry Rollins,
Who worked many hours editing this book. Waited patiently as REACH, and I, went through various incarnations. And never once failed to give his time and support over the years. Thanks.